"There's no reason you'd be a threat to anyone, is there?"

Gabby's eyes widened in either shock or outrage. "Of course not! In case you don't know, I was a complete failure as a witness."

Jack said quietly, "I'm sorry. I get used to asking nosy questions. I didn't mean to upset you."

"I'm not upset." She walked fast, keeping a distance between them.

He'd had to park farther away tonight; he could just as well have walked her back to the hotel, but he was glad she hadn't turned that way. They'd have had no privacy at all. She sure as hell wasn't going to invite him up to her room.

In his SUV, he started the engine but didn't reach to put on his seat belt. "I really am sorry. I was having a good time."

"I was, too," she said softly.

"Okay." He hadn't turned the lights on yet, and the sidewalk was momentarily deserted. He realized she was looking at him, her face a pale oval.

Before he thought it through, Jack leaned forward and kissed her.

COLD CASE FLASHBACKS

USA TODAY Bestselling Author

JANICE KAY JOHNSON

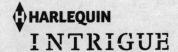

HARLEQUIN
INTRIGUE

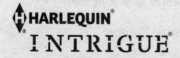

HARLEQUIN®
INTRIGUE®

ISBN-13: 978-1-335-40175-5

Cold Case Flashbacks

Copyright © 2021 by Janice Kay Johnson

Recycling programs
for this product may
not exist in your area.

This edition published by arrangement with Harlequin Books S.A.

For questions and comments about the quality of this book,
please contact us at CustomerService@Harlequin.com.

Harlequin Enterprises ULC
22 Adelaide St. West, 40th Floor
Toronto, Ontario M5H 4E3, Canada
www.Harlequin.com

Printed in U.S.A.

An author of more than ninety books for children and adults with more than seventy-five for Harlequin, **Janice Kay Johnson** writes about love and family, and pens books of gripping romantic suspense. A *USA TODAY* bestselling author and an eight-time finalist for the Romance Writers of America RITA® Award, she won a RITA® Award in 2008. A former librarian, Janice raised two daughters in a small town north of Seattle, Washington.

Books by Janice Kay Johnson

Harlequin Intrigue

Hide the Child
Trusting the Sheriff
Within Range
Brace for Impact
The Hunting Season
The Last Resort
Cold Case Flashbacks

Visit the Author Profile page at Harlequin.com.

CAST OF CHARACTERS

Gabriella Ortiz—Childhood witness to murder, Gabby returns to the town she hasn't seen since she was five years old. Hoping buried memories will resurface, she doesn't expect attempts on her life—or to fall for a man with a gift for lying.

Jack Cowan—A homicide detective obsessed with solving a very cold case, Jack is thrilled when the only witness to the murder returns to town twenty-five years later. But falling in love with her wasn't the plan, especially when keeping her alive becomes his priority.

Ric Ortiz—Gabby's brother, Ric, missed her, but also harbors anger toward her because she refuses to talk about what she saw.

Dean Keller—Now police chief, Dean was a hometown boy and readily okays the cold case investigation, but has secrets of his own.

Sergeant Rutkowski—Jack's boss, Rutkowski, knew Colleen Ortiz in high school. Is he too interested in every detail of the investigation?

Colleen Ortiz—A stay-at-home mother and the unlikeliest of victims, Colleen was brutally murdered in her own home.

Mark Cowan—A suspect in Colleen's murder, Mark is the reason for his son's obsession with the case. If only he'd told Jack everything he knows.

Chapter One

Jack Cowan investigated murderers, rapists and other scumbags on a daily basis, and was glad to snap the cuffs on each and every one of them. Not having it in his power to go after the killer he wanted most to nail…yeah, that ate at him.

Today Jack walked out of the locker room at the health club and saw Ric Ortiz on a treadmill. The one beside him was empty. Good. Ortiz was Jack's single remaining connection to the murdered woman and the one witness. That made him Jack's only hope, too.

The two men ran into each other often enough, Jack didn't have to orchestrate meetings. In a city the size of Leclaire, that happened. It was somewhere in the top twenty cities in Washington state by population and needed a significant police department, yet wasn't so big you didn't see people you knew at a grocery store or, in this case, a health club. Growing up, he and Ric had been school classmates and soccer and Little League teammates, thus sharing some parental carpools—before, in different ways, their worlds were shattered.

Even though he wanted to claim that empty treadmill before someone got to it, Jack paused to take a look around the gym with a cop's typical caution. He'd hit on a good hour to be here, he saw, with the place only half-full. Lots of machines available, weight lifters letting out harsh sounds and clanging the weights back onto the racks as they released them after their reps. He saw more women than men, some in formfitting exercise getups, but no one who caught his eye.

Unsettled by his complete lack of interest, he scanned some fine-looking female bodies again, but, damn, he just wanted to get in his run and go home. Eat and fall into bed, alone. He'd hook up with someone one of these days. It had been only… Okay, four or five months since he'd parted ways with Laura. Normally he'd have been getting restless, but he'd been working long hours, as detectives often did.

Jack reached the treadmill, adjusted the speed and set his water bottle in the holder before stepping onto the track. Ric Ortiz must have been there awhile, because he'd worked up a good sweat and was really moving. Tall and lean, he'd always been a good athlete.

He glanced at Jack, who started to jog. "How's it going?"

"Good." Jack had closed a big case yesterday and spent today on the paperwork. He'd intended to run at the park or on the high school track, but the sky started spitting out sleet as he left the police station and walked to his car. This was better than nothing. "You?"

The two men chatted desultorily. Ric's breath was coming hard and fast. Jack was only half listening when Ric said, out of the blue, "You remember my sister?" Not slowing, he snatched up a towel to wipe sweat from his face.

This was why Jack always made a point of talking to Ortiz when their paths crossed.

Still, as he stepped up his own speed, Jack only grunted a response.

In fact, he knew a hell of a lot more about Gabriella Ortiz than her brother could imagine. In Jack's most vivid memories of seeing the girl, she'd been riding a hot pink tricycle on the sidewalk outside the Ortiz home when Jack's mom dropped off Ric after a soccer practice or Little League. He pictured two dark pigtails tied off with pink ribbons. Either they were always pink or he just hadn't paid attention. Later, there'd been a bike with training wheels and more pink ribbons fluttering from the handlebars. Funny he could remember that, when he couldn't have cared less about some dumb little sister.

Not then.

But now he said with pretended indifference, "I remember you have a sister."

"Yeah, once upon a time." Seemingly brooding, Ric let his pace gradually drop. It was another couple of minutes before he said, "Gabby's coming home."

Gabby's coming home.

Jack broke stride, stumbled, cursed and had to do some quick footwork to keep from falling and to regain his pace.

Fortunately, Ric's head had turned as he answered a hail from some buddy. Gave Jack a minute to hide his shock and exultation.

"To stay?" he asked.

"To stay?" Ortiz glanced his way. "Oh, you mean Gabby. Uh, probably not. This is more of a visit. We haven't seen each other since, man, she was like eight and I was eleven."

"She went to live with an aunt, didn't she?" And had grown up in a smallish town in Vermont.

Ric slowed to a cooldown jog. "Dad and I flew back to see her a few times that first year or two, but my great-aunt wasn't what you'd call welcoming. I guess…even Dad kind of gave up." His forehead crinkled. "He thought she was better off there."

Safer, was what Ric meant. Supposedly, four-year-old Gabby had had a couple of near misses that might have been nothing, just weird things happening, but might instead have been attempts on her life. Gabby Ortiz had witnessed her mother's murder, so that made sense. Enough, at least, that Jack could see why her dad would have thought an out-of-sight, out-of-mind plan good.

Gabby now had to be almost thirty…no, she *was* thirty. Doing his research, Jack had taken note of her September birthday.

"What inspired the visit?" Jack asked.

Ric stepped off his treadmill and ran the towel over his head, leaving his dark hair sticking up in spikes.

"We've been emailing more often. With Dad gone now…" He shrugged.

Given his intense interest in the Ortiz family, Jack had noted the obituary in the local paper, too. He'd even gone to the funeral, wondering if prolonged grief had worn out Raul Ortiz's heart before its time.

"Great-Aunt Isabel died, I don't know, seven or eight years ago, too," Ric added. "One of Mom's sisters is still alive, as far as I know, but they were ten years apart in age and never close. I've barely met those cousins, and I doubt Gabby has at all. That kind of leaves the two of us."

"I know what you mean." Jack's sister was married to an army officer, and they were currently stationed in Jordan right now. Really, they were almost complete strangers. That left him and his father, and Dad was in Oregon.

Dad grieved, too. If his heart gave out, Jack wouldn't be surprised. Enraged, but not surprised.

"So… I get pissed at her," Ric said. "She should have come home years ago. Told the cops what she knows, but she didn't want to hear it. Buried her head in the sand and won't pull it out. We'd get friendly, then mad at each other and not be in contact for a year." His mouth tightened. "Not holding my breath, but I guess I'm hoping that seeing each other will mean something. You know?"

"I hope it does," Jack said sincerely, even as he was thinking about whether she'd talk to *him*.

"I gotta get going." Ric seemed to shake off his mood. "Good to see you."

"Yeah." As Ric walked away, Jack called, "Hey, when's she coming?"

The guy turned to walk backward. "Next week. Monday. We've been planning this for a while."

"Good luck."

"Yeah." The grin was kind of weak, and a minute later, Ric disappeared into the locker room.

Jack kicked up his speed and brooded. Be straight with her and ask for an official interview? That's what he should do, but what if she declined? Going undercover wasn't something he'd exactly done before, given the size of this town. Too much chance of being recognized. But she'd have no way of knowing about his obsession with her mother's murder, so it might not matter if she knew he was a cop. He could sound her out a little, find out what she was like. Why she hadn't come home, even once she was an adult and her aunt had died.

Her confused childhood memories might be gone altogether, but if so, wouldn't you think she'd have told her brother? If they were still there, in her head, why was she refusing to examine them? Maybe knowing what Jack did for a living might be a positive, if she had any desire at all to talk about the stalled investigation and whatever weird stuff surfaced in nightmares.

Or maybe she barely remembered her mother and figured what was past, was past. She'd moved on with her life.

Well, there were people who hadn't, he thought, speared by bitterness and anger, and she owed them something. He had every intention of making sure she paid.

"RIC?" GABBY WOULDN'T have recognized the man pushing himself away from a pillar near baggage claim at the Spokane International Airport if she didn't follow him on Instagram and a couple of other sites. Not until he smiled did she see the skinny boy she'd worshipped as a kid.

"Damn." He grinned at her. "Who'd have thought you'd come out looking so good?"

She made a face and surrendered her laptop case to him. He leaned over to kiss her cheek.

"Didn't grow so much, though, did you?" he added, reminding her how much he had loved irritating her.

She sniffed. "Doesn't take mass to make quality."

His laugh followed her to the carousel, where bags were appearing. She could have packed enough in a carry-on suitcase…but on the chance she'd decide to extend her stay, Gabby had decided to bring plenty.

Feeling a certain queasiness at the thought, she reminded herself that, for all her determination to find some answers, she wasn't stuck here. She could pack up and leave whenever she wanted. Who could stop her? She just…didn't want to hurt her brother's feelings. Or close off any possibility of a relationship with him.

Leclaire was a western suburb of Spokane, almost butting up to the Washington–Idaho border. The drive from the airport shouldn't take long. Once Ric had loaded her and her bags and they got on the way, she didn't recognize a thing. She could have been on the outskirts of any medium-size city in the US, except this one was greener than most. She saw some forests and low mountains in the distance, and that had to be the Spokane River.

"Look familiar?" Ric asked.

She shook her head. "I was so young. I wish Mom and Dad had been into camping or something like that, but…" She shrugged. "I remember the house and the neighborhood, sort of, but not much else."

His dark eyes rested on her face for a minute, but she resisted meeting them. She knew what he was thinking. *Don't you remember watching Mom get butchered?*

A rush of adrenaline made childish feelings well up in her. *I don't! I don't!* But she kept her mouth clamped shut. That argument never went well. Ric must be trying, and she'd do the same. She had to face the fact that, however hard she tried to recover her memories, she might fail. She'd worked too hard to *block* those memories. To be a strong woman, how could she build on the shaky foundation of knowing, in the most terrifying way, what true vulnerability felt like?

Anyway, the murder had happened so many years ago, and she'd seen it as young child, not an adult. Kids didn't think the same. Plus her mind might have reworked the memories and even her ability to access them in order to allow her to recover and become a functioning person.

Yes, the visit would bring back memories. Enough to be helpful? She had no idea. And she didn't plan to tell Ric she was going to try to do as he asked until she found out whether she could get anywhere. Their perspectives were poles apart.

For starters, she couldn't understand how Ric had brought himself to stay in their childhood home. Since he wasn't married, it was too big for him. And Dad. How had *he* stood living there, where Mom had been murdered? Did he have to clean up her blood himself? Why hadn't he moved? Wouldn't that have been healthier for Ric?

And maybe the biggest question was, why hadn't Dad been willing to move so he could keep *both* of his children with him?

Yeah, she had her issues.

The silence had become prolonged. Her fault. She sifted through possibilities and went with, "So, are you seeing anyone right now?"

"Not seriously," he admitted. "What about you?"

"No." She wasn't sure she could do serious. That was one of those issues. "I date, but…" She shrugged.

"Job?"

Keep it light. "I don't have much staying power." She was one dissertation away from her PhD in American History, but once that was approved, she'd be looking for a position at a university where she'd be put on a tenure track and maybe never leave. The idea made her shiver. The reasons for her procrastination on polishing the blasted dissertation and presenting it were not subtle.

Nor relevant, she reminded herself. This was a visit, that's all. Whether she could come up with any information to help track her mother's murderer or not, this wasn't home anymore. She'd get to know Ric, but not too well. His turn to visit her next. Somewhere, anywhere, besides the city and house that were bound to keep haunting her.

At the sight of a bright green highway sign that said Leclaire, Gabby leaned forward, stretching out the seat belt.

"Four exits?"

"It's grown." Ric put on the turn signal and worked his way two lanes to the right, finally leaving the freeway.

"Oh, I made a reservation at the Wilmont," she said. "I don't think it's that far from the house."

He braked at a red light and turned to stare at her. "What? You're not staying with me?"

"I... I thought it might be more comfortable for both of us not to be thrown together quite that much."

"Is it the house? Or me?"

Oh, heavens, she'd already hurt his feelings.

"Mostly the house, but...a little bit of both. I don't *know* you. Every time I think I start to, you lash out at me." She swallowed. Pride kept her voice even. "I thought some space would make sense."

"Fine." He accelerated hard enough to press her back in her seat. "I'll give you all the space you want."

"You're mad at me."

"You think?"

Of course, he was. She should have told him in advance. But why would he imagine she'd cheerfully go home with him to her childhood bedroom? Hang out in the kitchen, when he had to guess she'd look like a kid playing hopscotch to be sure she didn't step on the place where Mom's body had lain, or plant a foot in the pools of blood?

He hadn't been home. *He* hadn't seen Mom's body at all. Probably not even the blood. So what did he know?

She clamped her jaw shut, gripped the seat belt crossing her chest and didn't say a word.

JACK HELD BACK until Tuesday, then called Ric. As if they were good enough friends. "Just wanted to say I hope the reunion is going well." He made it casual. "I kept thinking about you and Gabby."

"It's…not going so well." Ric sounded strange. "I shouldn't have assumed she'd want to stay with me, but I did. I didn't take it well when she asked me to drop her at a hotel."

"You blew up at her?"

"Not that bad." Ric sighed. "We had a really awkward dinner at the restaurant in the hotel. I haven't talked to her today."

"Where's she staying?" He caught himself. "I mean, she's here in town, right?"

"Oh, sure. The Wilmont. I know I need to talk to her, but how are we supposed to get to be friends if all we do is have a few restaurant meals?"

That was a really good question. "You know snow is being forecast."

"Why didn't she come when the leaves were changing and the weather was dry and crisp?"

Another good question. "Did she have a winter

break from a job?" Like her job teaching at a community college? The one he shouldn't know about?

Except, come to think of it, this was mid-November. Thanksgiving was next week, which made it too early for school breaks.

"Maybe." Ric's tone eased. "Yeah, that's probably it, but she didn't sound enthusiastic about what she's been doing. She didn't *say* she'd quit, but I wonder."

"Yeah? Where's she been living?"

"Oh, New Hampshire. Concord Community College. Actually, that's the second—no, third—college where she's taught since she finished grad school. Supposedly she's working on her dissertation, but she didn't seem all that interested in talking about it."

"She say how long she plans to stay here?"

"I was careful not to push it." Ric grunted. "It was like a really bad first date. You know, when conversation never takes off. Except in our case, there's this history. I kept looking at her and thinking, she's my little sister. I used to pull her pigtail or steal this stuffed hippopotamus she wouldn't go to bed without. Only… I can't make the two pictures merge."

Part of Jack sympathized, and part of him was afraid Gabby Ortiz would decide to leave town before he had a chance to talk to her at all. This might be his only chance.

"There's a lot of years in between," he pointed out. "Me, I was picturing this little girl with plump cheeks who always wore pink scooting up and down the sidewalk on that plastic tricycle. Like she was waiting for you."

"I think she was."

"Listen, I was off today, just stayed home because the weather stinks. How about if I take the two of you out? Fancy, if you think she'd like that, but we could just go for pizza and beer. Maybe having someone else with you would lower the pressure."

"You'd do that?" Ric sounded surprised, and for good reason, considering they were more acquaintances these days than friends.

"Why not? I think what happened to your mother was one of the reasons I went into law enforcement. What Gabby saw back then—" He cleared his throat. "I wouldn't mind seeing her, all grown up."

"Man, if you mean that, it would be great. That is, if she's okay with it. I can't think of any of her friends who are still around here, but even the couple guys who were at my house the most often are long gone. Not that she probably remembers them anyway."

"Why don't you check with her?" Jack suggested, sounding a lot more casual than he felt.

"I'll do that and get back to you."

If she said no? Jack fully intended to find a plan B.

Chapter Two

"All right. What's this about?" Chief Keller asked brusquely.

Jack's sergeant had walked up to the office with him, having given his provisional approval for the request. But he decided they needed permission from above. As soon as Jack had firmed plans for dinner with Ric and Gabby this evening, he'd driven straight to the station.

Now, Sergeant Rutkowski stayed silent, leaving Jack to say, "I'd like permission to open a cold case."

Dean Keller had risen through the ranks and was respected within the department. Since Jack rarely had anything to do with the chief, he couldn't claim to know him, or guess how he'd react to an upstart detective thinking he could accomplish something his predecessors hadn't. Solving Colleen Ortiz's high-profile murder. Leclaire Police Department's failure to make an arrest had been a black mark in the eyes of the public.

Keller studied Jack keenly. "What's your interest?"

"I read about it when I first came on board," Jack

said. He hesitated, then admitted, "My father was an initial suspect in Mrs. Ortiz's murder. He talked about it."

The chief's expression changed. "Cowan." Then, more slowly, "Brian Cowan. I remember the name. I was a patrol officer at the time. Does your father still live locally?"

"No, he's in Bend, Oregon."

"What would he think of this idea?"

Jack had no idea. Dad had long since resigned himself to his many losses in a way Jack wasn't willing to do. "I didn't discuss it with him. I have to believe he'd be glad if Mrs. Ortiz's murderer was arrested."

Keller's gaze shifted to Sergeant Rutkowski. "What do you think?"

"He's got a chance that may not come along again. Cowan has a hell of a closure rate. You know that. I'd have chosen him to take something like this on." He shrugged. "The timing is good. Major crime usually drops when people are stuck at home because of snow or ice."

"What's this 'chance'?" the chief asked sharply.

Jack answered, "You may recall that Mrs. Ortiz's daughter witnessed the killing."

"Good God, she was a toddler! From what I heard, her testimony—if you can even call it that—was worthless."

"She was four and a half. Actually, closer to five. Kids are pretty verbal by that age." They sure as hell knew their colors. Gabriella Ortiz had insisted the man had worn all blue. "They start learning to read.

She was traumatized. I'm hoping that she remembers something she was afraid to say then, or as a young child didn't understand but now does."

"If so, why hasn't she come to us?"

"Again, the event was pretty traumatic. She may have been encouraged to block out what she did remember, especially if it was giving her nightmares."

"And this woman lives…where? Are you expecting the department to fund your travels?"

"No, sir." He knew how tight the budget was. "I happened to learn that Ms. Ortiz is here in Leclaire for a visit. Her brother still lives here."

"Huh." Chief Keller leaned back in his desk chair, rubbed a hand over his jaw and brooded for a minute. "Can you keep this reasonably quiet?"

"I can't control Gabrielle Ortiz or her brother, Ric, should they decide to go to the press. I think that's pretty unlikely, though." He decided not to mention that Ric had been hot to reopen the case for years. Since he wouldn't know Jack was reopening it, at least for the time being, Jack didn't see a problem. "Ric and I went to high school together, both played football and baseball. I happened to run into him a week or so ago, and that's when he told me about his sister's visit. I figure it's at least worth sitting down with her."

The sergeant didn't say anything. Jack stayed physically relaxed, despite the determination that simmered at a near boil. Had to appear intrigued but dispassionate. He was curious, that's all.

"Okay," Keller said. "We may have to cut you off if we get too busy or if it's obvious you aren't getting anywhere, but we'd all like to see this one closed. It's worth a try."

"Thank you, sir." Jack rose from the chair, nodded and walked out, waiting in the outer office for the sergeant, who'd paused to exchange a few words with the chief.

Both men nodded at Chief Keller's assistant and continued to the elevator together. Jack pushed the button. While they waited, Rutkowski said, "Didn't expect a problem. I really hope you get somewhere with her."

"I do, too," Jack said with complete sincerity— and no intention of admitting that he was making the initial approach to Gabby Ortiz as neighborhood kid grown up, a casual friend of her brother's, not as a homicide detective with his eye on her as a witness.

Testing the waters, that's all. Going with his instinct, which said that a woman who'd refused to come back to town for twenty-five years wouldn't immediately open up to an investigator who demanded she mine her most painful memories.

Even when he did tell her he was reopening the case, he could claim he'd just decided to do it. That he'd had an ulterior motive all along…well, why would she ever have to find that out?

RIC HAD SUGGESTED an Italian restaurant only six blocks from Gabby's hotel. Of course he offered to pick her up, but the Wilmont offered free Uber service within downtown, so she said she'd meet them there.

Them.

Having arrived before the two men and been seated in a booth, Gabby let herself wonder why Ric was bringing someone else. It didn't sound like this Jack Cowan was a really close friend, but she did remember the name. She even thought she could picture him, a tall boy with ruffled brown hair that must have had some curl. Later, though, Dad had sent her articles from the local newspaper about the successes of both Ric's high school baseball and football teams. Ric had pitched, Jack had been the first baseman. On the football field, Jack was the quarterback who'd led the team to a state championship, Ric his favorite wide receiver. Gabby had hungrily studied the couple photos of her brother, but only one photo of Jack Cowan lingered in her memory. They'd been seniors the year their football team went all the way, so she would have been…thirteen. No, probably fourteen. Definitely boy crazy. She'd thought Jack's broad, triumphant grin was sexy. She'd thought *he* was sexy. The idea was laughable now, given how skinny he'd undoubtedly been, how immature.

Still…having him here might ease the tension between her and Ric, who'd had more expectations of her than she could handle. Wow, if he had any idea she intended to try to do what he'd long demanded of her, he'd turn into a bulldozer and drive her nuts.

Sipping her glass of water, she was facing the door when Ric and another man walked in. A group of three women at a nearby table turned their heads in unison. Gabby didn't blame them. She felt appreciation for a fine sight.

Ric was really good-looking, his Latino heritage showing in near-black hair and dark eyes. The height came from Mom's side of the family. Jack Cowan had a craggier face, not as obviously handsome, but there was something elementally male in that big, broad-shouldered body and the saunter that seemed unconscious.

She lifted a hand, Ric spotted her and said something to his friend, who looked straight at her and changed his path between tables. She wasn't sure his eyes ever left hers until… He arrived at the booth, he stood looking down at her.

His medium brown hair, cut short, was still unruly, and his eyes were a bright blue.

Then he grinned. "I'd never have recognized you."

"You remember me?"

"Yeah, you had that pink tricycle you'd pedal up and down the sidewalk."

Gabby wrinkled her nose at him. She'd loved all things pink at that age, had even thrown a temper tantrum if Mom wanted her to wear any other color, except occasionally purple.

"No more pink," he added.

To her puzzlement, he kept standing there, his assessment unexpectedly…thorough. After a moment, he glanced toward the front of the restaurant, then the nearby hall leading to the restrooms and kitchen. Her brother raised his eyebrows, edged by him and sat beside her.

At last, Jack sat, too, but slid all the way across and relaxed against the wall, half-facing them and half-facing the room. "A pitcher?" he suggested, lifting a hand for an approaching waiter.

"Gabby?" her brother asked.

"That's fine." She didn't love beer, but wine and pizza would be ridiculous. And, really, she wasn't much of a drinker at all. Great-Aunt Isabel hadn't approved of "spirits."

Jack Cowan went back to studying her as Ric ordered the pitcher. "You look good," he said after a minute.

Something about the intensity in his gaze unsettled her—or maybe it was her reaction to him. "Did you expect terrible?"

He laughed. "I guess that was rude. I just expected…" He hesitated. "Chubby cheeks."

Oh, lord—she'd been plump back then, to put it kindly. Mom said she had chipmunk cheeks. In pictures where she was beaming, her eyes ended up squinty in that fat face. *She'd* expected to grow up with chubby cheeks, like the women on Dad's side of the family. Instead, she had apparently acquired her mother's fine bones and ivory skin. Not Mom's height, though, or warm brown hair; nope, Gabby's was black, thick and stubbornly straight.

One side of Jack's mouth turned up. "You and Ric look like brother and sister."

"Except for the foot difference in height." Her brother just couldn't help rubbing it in. "Not to mention some actual muscles."

She lifted her chin. "I exercise. I just don't admire myself in mirrors while I sculpt unnecessary muscles."

Jack gave a crack of laughter, and even Ric grinned.

"Sharp-tongued little thing," he observed.

Amusement still lingering on his face, Jack said, "I like that in a woman."

She was terribly afraid her cheeks heated.

They settled down to choosing a pizza, a giant one. The men considered ordering two, but she reminded them that she, at least, wouldn't be taking any leftovers. Irritation crossed Ric's face. Jack's eyes flickered as he took that in. He was exceptionally observant, she couldn't help thinking.

Once the pitcher arrived and he'd poured glasses of beer for all three of them, he said, "Ric tells me you're a college professor."

"Well…halfway. I've been taking lecturer positions at two-year colleges while I work on my dissertation. My chances of getting on at a good four-year school are zilch until I have the PhD."

"History?"

"Yes. One of those majors that does not lead to sky-high salaries."

He laughed again. She really liked what that laugh did to his face. "We have that in common. I'm a cop."

She froze, the glass almost to her lips. A cop? Why hadn't Ric told her? Pulling herself together, she took a sip of beer to give herself a moment. Was he someone she could talk to, if she got to that point?

"Yeah? Did you get a degree in criminology?"

She congratulated herself on sounding no more than pleasantly interested.

"I did. Went to Portland State. My dad moved to Oregon my senior year in high school. I stayed here with a friend's family until I graduated."

"And came back once you had your degree?"

His big shoulders moved. "It's home."

Her brother didn't seem to recognize any awkwardness. Sounding smug, he said, "I'll bet I out-earn you both."

She stuck out her tongue.

Jack grimaced. "Safe to say."

A mechanical engineer, her brother worked for a company known for their specialty tools. He hadn't told Gabby how much he made, but it had to be plenty—certainly enough for him to have bought a different house.

But, no, Ric had gone to Washington State University here in Eastern Washington, and was now on his second job in Spokane, an easy commute from Leclaire. None of that was chance. Of course, Dad had kept *him*, and this was his home, as it was Jack Cowan's. And Ric and she had experienced Mom's murder and the aftermath in completely different ways.

Which reminded her... "Are you with Leclaire PD?" she asked Jack. Seeing his nod, she asked, "What do you do with the department?"

"Started out at the bottom, took the detective exam a few years back and I'm now assigned to major crimes. I wrapped up an ugly home invasion and rape case just recently, for example."

Ric hoisted his glass. "I read about that. I didn't realize you were the investigator."

"I was."

"That must be…hard," she murmured. "I mean, seeing what you do."

SEEING WHAT SHE HAD. That had to be what she was thinking.

"Sometimes," he agreed, his gaze holding hers even as he braced himself. Lying on the job was often necessary, but lying to this woman…

I am *on the job,* he reminded himself, still not happy about looking into her eyes and saying, *Nope, I barely remember your mother's murder. And you? A witness? Wow, nobody told me.*

No, she wouldn't buy that.

"You know about our mother," she said flatly.

"Yeah, I do." He tried to make his tone gentle as he picked his way through the minefield. "Ric and I were friends, teammates. How could I not? In fact, I told Ric the other day, I think what happened to your mom and your family is part of what motivated me to consider law enforcement for a career. Becoming a detective was always my goal. People forget that a murder sends out ripples of pain. Family and friends becomes victims, too, in a sense. I can't claim to understand, but even as a kid I could see it happening to your family."

She swallowed and looked away. After a moment, she nodded. "Can we not talk about it?"

"Always your solution," her brother mumbled.

"This isn't exactly the time or place," she snapped.

Her green-gold eyes already held Jack's attention. Now a flare of pain or anger or both accentuated the gold.

Damn. He hadn't anticipated his attraction to this woman—the woman he intended to deceive and, eventually, press for every painful memory she'd buried.

And he couldn't kid himself. He wouldn't be doing it for her. He wanted to shame every person who'd ever looked with doubt at his father.

Because his own family had been broken by Colleen Ortiz's murder, too. And if Gabby remembered anything, she owed all the other people who'd been hurt to lay it out in the light of day.

But she was right. This wasn't the moment for that. Instead, Jack set out to tamp down the tension between sister and brother.

"My fault the subject came up. Hey, I hope that's our pizza. I'm starved."

"Because you slaved all day?" Ric mocked him, apparently willing to go along.

"Yeah, that was me."

Once the pizza was in front of them and Ric was handing out plates, Jack continued, "Lounged on my couch in sweats and watched a Seahawks game I missed." True as far as it went.

The beautiful woman sitting on the other side of

the booth looked askance at him. "But you must know how it came out."

"Well, sure." He let her take a slice, then dished up a bigger one for himself. "But I wanted to see more than the highlights."

She rolled her eyes. "I mean, I follow the NFL. But it's no fun once you know who has won or lost."

Jack narrowed his eyes. "Please don't tell me you're a fan of the—" He couldn't even say it.

"The Patriots? Of course I am. I live in New England."

Making a strangled sound, he fell back in pretended anguish.

Her brother laughed. "I should have warned you."

They moved on to talking and arguing about a dozen topics while devouring the pizza. Well, she stopped after two slices, but he and Ric took care of the rest. Nobody would be taking any home.

Ric insisted on handling the bill, smirking as he reminded them of their relative poverty. As they walked out, he offered her a ride back to the hotel, but she shook her head with a smile and held up her phone.

"I already sent for the Uber."

Ric zipped up his coat, pulled on gloves and started down the sidewalk. Zipping up his own parka, Jack raised his brows.

"You lied."

"I didn't… How do you know?" she demanded, her indignation obvious.

"I was walking behind you."

"Hmph. Well, I'm going to do it right now."

"Why don't you let me drop you? My car is only half a block away."

Her teeth closed on her lower lip as she hesitated, then finally nodded. "Thanks. I'm at the Wilmont."

"Ric told me."

"He's mad."

"He told me that, too."

They set out down the sidewalk together, Jack shortening his steps. She probably wasn't more than five foot two or three inches at the most. At least she'd come dressed for the weather, probably not surprising for someone accustomed to Vermont winters. No, wait—currently New Hampshire. Couldn't be much different.

With half a dozen restaurants and upscale bars in a two-block span, there was quite a bit of pedestrian traffic, enough that he laid a hand on Gabby's back briefly when a group spilling out of a door engulfed them.

He unlocked his Tahoe from a distance away, then opened the passenger door and hovered behind her until she'd climbed up to the seat before going around to his side. As he started the engine and turned down the fan until the heat cranked up, he said, "It's early here for such crap weather."

"It's been cold in New Hampshire, too."

Interesting she hadn't said "back home" or the like. After pulling out into traffic, he asked how long she planned to stay.

"I...haven't decided. I guess it depends how things go with Ric."

"What about your job?" Her timing was definitely odd, whether her college was on a quarter or semester system.

She stole a sidelong look. "I haven't told Ric yet, but I quit after the fall quarter. They'd only offered me two classes for winter quarter. It depends on enrollment, you see. Being part-time means no benefits—"

"And no living wage."

"Right. So I figured this was a good time to make myself finish the damn dissertation."

He found himself smiling. "Don't you have to present it in person? I hope you summon a little more enthusiasm than that for the profs."

Gabby had a great laugh, a ripple of humor that felt like fingertips dancing over his chest. "I'll try."

The hotel was coming up. *Give it a shot.*

"Listen," he said, "I've enjoyed myself tonight. I don't know if you're reserving all your time for Ric, but if not… I'd like to take you out. Say, dinner tomorrow." Or the next day. Any day.

"Oh."

He glided to the curb and braked. A doorman appeared in the gilt-trimmed glass doors into the hotel. Time was running out.

"I'd like that." She sounded shy. "Tomorrow would be great."

His triumph was mixed with a hint of guilt—but he'd take what he could get anyway.

Chapter Three

"Someone tried to break into my house last night."

Phone to his ear, Jack straightened abruptly in his desk chair in the detective bullpen. "What the hell?"

Fellow detectives at neighboring desks were on the phone—probably on hold—hammering on their computer keyboards or huddled in conversation. None of them even turned their head at his exclamation.

Ric Ortiz said, "You heard me. I mean, sure, the neighborhood has an occasional break-in, the kind where the TV and iPod get stolen. But at night? When chances are good a resident is home?"

"Were you parked in the driveway?"

"Garage."

"What happened?"

"Pure luck," Ric said grimly. "A neighbor was coming home, saw the motion-activated floodlight was on in back. The guy probably heard the car engine and the sound of the garage door opening. Could be, it even sounded like it was at my house. Anyway, Chuck saw a dark figure running between my house and the one to the north and up the sidewalk. He called 9-1-1."

"So you did report it."

"Oh, yeah. For what good that did. Officer pretty much shrugged and said it happens. He drove around a little bit, but of course the guy was long gone."

"It does happen," Jack said automatically, even though he was disturbed. For one thing, *he'd* grown up in that part of town, about a mile from the Ortiz home. But more than that…

"You told many people your sister's back in Leclaire?" he asked.

The silence suggested surprise…or that Ric had been thinking the same, however subliminally.

"Quite a few," he said after a minute. "No reason not to tell my friends and some of the neighbors who were here then. I ran into Mr. Corcoran, too—remember him?"

High school principal. Of course Jack remembered him. Corcoran was now the district superintendent.

"And I guess I've seen a few of Mom and Dad's friends," Ric added.

In other words, word would have spread like wildfire among those who remembered the brutal crime.

"Does anybody know she's not staying with you?"

This silence was different. It was followed by a curse. "No," Ric said. "You don't really think—"

"I actually don't." Truth. "It was probably a dumb teenager after some electronics or cash. Dark house, thought he could sneak in and out unseen. I'm just being paranoid. Occupational hazard."

"I can see how you'd get like that." Ric sounded relieved.

"All the same…" He hesitated. "If you haven't told anyone where she's staying, don't."

"I haven't wanted to admit she's not staying at the house." Gabby's brother sighed. "Yeah, okay. Should I tell her what happened?"

Jack mulled that over. "Ah…why don't you let me."

"You have her number?"

"I do." Whether this was a good idea or bad, he had no clue, but if he didn't tell her brother, Gabby would. "I'm actually having dinner with her tonight. I hope you don't mind."

Ric muttered something Jack didn't catch. Probably just as well. Then, "Gabby has made it pretty clear I don't have anything to say about her life."

"She's here in town. To see *you*. Don't knock it."

After a few more grumbly sounds, Ric said, "She *is* my sister. Watch it with her," and ended the call.

Jack set down his phone to brood for a minute before focusing again on his current investigation.

Not twenty minutes later, his sergeant stopped by his desk. "What are you working on?"

Jack tore his eyes off his computer monitor to focus on Rutkowski. "The large equipment stolen from the WKB construction site."

It was the dollar amount attached to the bulldozer, forklift and other equipment that had resulted in the theft being bumped up to his caseload.

The sergeant scowled. "Has to be an inside job. Or even an insurance scam."

"I agree." He nodded toward his computer. "I'm looking into the contractor's finances right now."

A short nod expressed approval. "Get any start on the Ortiz murder?"

Jack glanced around but saw no sign anyone had heard the name. And after Ric had told so many people about Gabby's return, keeping this investigation quiet probably wouldn't fly. Still, he'd rather try.

"Had a casual meeting yesterday. Because I was friends with her brother, I was able to get away with not telling her yet what I'm planning. Figured if she's comfortable with me, she'd be more likely to open up later."

"You going to be able to separate her from the brother?"

"I'm working on it."

"Keep me informed."

"There's no urgency, is there?"

Rutkowski shrugged. "Chief asked."

Watching the sergeant walk across the squad room to his office, Jack wasn't pleased to have caught Chief Keller's interest and attention. He'd hoped to keep this investigation low-key.

He *would* keep the investigation low-key, he vowed. This was his idea, he'd been given the go-ahead, and it was unlikely anyone in the command structure would second-guess him. If they did…he'd fight back.

Satisfied, he returned his attention to the credit report he'd been studying.

TWO BLOCKS AWAY from the house, Gabby realized how fast she was breathing. She didn't have the excuse of having run across town. Nope, she'd driven.

She braked at the corner, glad there was no other traffic. She'd decided this morning to rent a car rather than rely entirely on taxis or Ubers—or her brother. This gave her the freedom to drive around the town of which she had only hazy memories, and to start exploring her childhood without pressure from anyone else.

A department store downtown in a tall granite building accented with elaborately carved flat stones was definitely familiar. It had been a Macy's. Mom had loved to browse there more than actually make purchases. Target now occupied the building—not quite the same thing.

She recognized a burger place with a drive-through that wasn't part of a chain, too. Yes, they'd gone there once in a while as a big treat. Her family hadn't had a lot of money.

Otherwise, not much looked familiar. That was partly because the town had changed drastically in twenty-five years, and partly because she'd been so young when she left. A four-year-old didn't pay much attention to landmarks or stores. She pictured herself in the cart at a grocery store, begging for something she desperately wanted, but had no idea what that had been, whether Mom had bought it or what store it was then.

As she'd driven past the stores, no memories had upset her, so she'd felt confident about going by the house. She'd pictured it—but chances were good it had been painted half a dozen times at least, Dad or Ric might have built a new front porch, added a bay window or who knew what. She might not even recognize it.

Except, here she sat at a stop sign, on the verge of chickening out. She could do this another day, or wait and have Ric take her.

No, not that, because he'd want her to go inside, and she wasn't ready for that.

Okay, Jack. He'd probably be willing to drive by with her.

No, damn it. Gabby refused to depend on someone else—especially a man she hardly knew—to do something so…ordinary. She was stronger than that. She didn't even have to think about what happened to Mom, not yet. Just scope out the home where she'd spent hours at a time playing in the front yard or riding that plastic trike up and down the sidewalk until she knew every crack, every tree that overhung it.

She could do this.

She lifted her foot and let the car roll across the intersection. Yes, the neighborhood was familiar. Houses all dated to the same era, 1940s at a guess. Some were boxy, a few a classier bungalow-style with porches that went all the way across the front and square pillars supporting the roof and arched trimming. Several homes on this block had picket fences, as, she saw ahead, did ones in the next block.

Her block.

These were nice family homes. A few might be

rented, but all were so well kept, she guessed they were mostly owner occupied. Lawns were brown, of course, the grass probably crisp from the well-below-freezing temperatures. Big old trees, maples and cherries and oaks, looked sculptural with no leaves.

This cross street had no stop sign. Lucky there wasn't any other traffic, or kids out riding bikes, because her gaze had locked on a house halfway down the block on the left.

The Ortiz home was one of the plain farmhouse-style ones. If Dad or Ric had done any remodeling, it didn't show from the outside. The picket fence almost had to have been replaced at some point, but it looked identical, painted white. The arbor over the gated walk from the sidewalk was draped with thick thorny stems of a climbing rose bush. The blooms, she knew, were a deep pink, and fragrant.

Her heart was pounding so hard, once she braked at the curb across the street from her childhood home, she pressed the heel of her hand hard against her chest.

A memory superimposed itself over the reality. Her pink plastic tricycle sat in the driveway near a bike that lay on its side, a helmet slung over the handlebars. Daddy got mad at both of them if he had to get out of his car to move bikes out of the way before he could drive into the garage. He *'specially* got annoyed at Ric, who was old enough to know better.

Why was she across the street looking at the house? Mommy said *never* to cross. *Never* to step into the street. Gabby was always supposed to stay in sight of the front windows, too. She was big enough to look for traffic before she started back across, but too late. Mommy burst out the front door.

Whimpering, Gabby sloughed off the memory and saw that the front door was painted red, just like it always had been even though the house had been white trimmed with black.

It still was.

The anger she felt at her brother swelled until she felt as if it would split her skin. Was Ric *nuts*? Did he think if he didn't change a single thing, time would magically replay itself? Well, even if it did, *he* hadn't been there to change a single thing.

Oh, dear God. If they'd replaced the kitchen floor, had they bought vinyl with the exact same pattern? She saw it, a black-and-white checkerboard, flowing with blood as shiny and red as the front door.

With a groan, she put the car back into gear and pulled away from the curb. Eyes glazed by tears, she drove a few blocks before she stopped again to mop her face and regain her composure.

How could Ric live there? And how could he *imagine* she'd be willing to walk in the door, far less stay there with him?

What had she been thinking to come back to Leclaire at all?

If she wasn't having dinner with Jack Cowan tonight, she'd have been hugely tempted to go straight back to the hotel, go online and buy an airline ticket out of there, even if it meant Ric never spoke to her again.

So much for the calm determination to find answers she'd started out with. Was it even possible to overcome trauma that occurred when a child was as young as she'd been?

She had no idea.

"What?" Jack's words ricocheted in her head. If she hadn't gone by the house today, she might not be so shocked. As it was…a chill crawled over her skin, as if she'd walked outside without her wool coat.

Jack was watching her with those too-discerning eyes. "Ric was really disturbed by the break-in. If the neighbor hadn't happened to come home at the right time…"

Her brother might have woken up to the sound of the floorboards creaking outside his bedroom…or even the squeak of his bedroom door opening.

"Why didn't he call me?" That was one of the questions tangling in her mind.

"I said I'd let you know." Now Jack looked wary. "I, uh, told him I was seeing you tonight."

Uh-oh. "What did he say?"

He smiled. "To watch myself."

Gabby made a face. "He hardly knows me. It's kind of ridiculous for him to go big brother on me."

"Maybe it's even more natural for him. He still thinks of you as a child, the one he was supposed to watch out for."

She tipped her head. "Do you have sisters or brothers? I don't remember Ric ever saying."

They were at a Thai restaurant tonight, only a

couple of blocks from her hotel. Leclaire had a nice downtown, but it wasn't large.

He wiped any expression from his face. "A younger sister. After my parents divorced, she went with Mom, I stayed with Dad. I haven't seen her in years."

Gabby opened her mouth then closed it. If he wanted to tell her what had split his family so irrevocably, he would—but the very lack of expression said the subject was taboo.

"I drove by the house today," she blurted.

He dropped the mask again to let her see concern. "Did you remember it?"

"Too well." She told him that neither her father nor brother had changed anything about the house. Not the paint color, not the landscaping, not new windows. "It's creepy."

"Yeah," he said slowly. "I can see why you'd feel that way. Sometimes I wonder—"

He stopped so suddenly, she almost heard the squeal of brakes.

She'd respect some walls he threw up, but there was a limit. "What do you wonder?"

Lines on his forehead and even between his nose and mouth deepened, making him even less conventionally handsome, and yet… Gabby saw something that made her pulse accelerate.

He set down his fork and his eyes met hers. "Whether coming back to Leclaire was a healthy choice for me."

"Because you weren't happy here."

"Oh." His big shoulders shrugged and some of

the careworn expression eased. "I was and I wasn't. School was good. I was a jock, and I liked being a star." This grin had to be genuine. "Home…that was harder."

She nodded. "I never let myself wonder why Ric stayed. I mean, he could have gotten a job anywhere. It's not like he had any family left here."

Jack stayed quiet, letting her pursue her thought. "If he'd sold the place, bought another one, or even remodeled the damn house, I'd think he just liked Leclaire. As it is…" She shook her head. "I guess he can't move on."

A nerve jerked in Jack's cheek, and she guessed he was thinking he hadn't been able to move on, either. Except she had no idea what his issue was. *His* mother hadn't been murdered in his childhood home.

"Maybe you should ask him about it," Jack suggested. "It might only be that he sees the house as a trust, like he has to preserve it in your mom's memory or because your dad asked him to. Or maybe he feels less lonely there."

Gabby couldn't decide if the idea was comforting or, once again, just plain creepy.

"Hey." He reached across the table and laid his hand over hers, gently squeezing. "You did come home to get to know him."

She scrunched up her nose. "I was thinking more, we're adults now, can we be friends? There is zero point in trying to time travel."

Her vehemence might explain the flare of something in his eyes, but it might not, too.

"Your mom's killer was never caught," he said.

"So Ric keeps pointing out." Hearing how acidly that had come out, she closed her eyes for a moment. "I'm sorry. I shouldn't take my annoyance with him out on you. Do you think we can talk about something else?"

"Sure." Jack smiled. "Please tell me you don't have a boyfriend back in New Hampshire."

"No, if I did I might not have quit my job and made this…pilgrimage." Heavens, was that what this trip was? "What about you?"

"Give me some credit. If I were seeing anyone, I wouldn't have asked you out for dinner tonight."

"Have you been married?"

"Never even come close." He shrugged. "There are women who like the idea of dating a cop. The reality always turns out to sour them. Nobody likes being stood up over and over again."

"You think that's the problem?"

He grinned wickedly. "What else could it be?"

She laughed at him. His ego wasn't suffering. "I wouldn't dare guess."

"So, what's your excuse?"

That was a better question than she wanted to admit. "Does a woman my age need to have an excuse for not getting married? Maybe I'm not ready." How could a woman who couldn't even commit to a long-term job *be* ready? "Maybe I like my independence."

He bent his head toward her. "Both good reasons. So tell me more about you. How was living with your great-aunt?"

"Hard when I was so young. She was…stern. I really grew to love her, though, and I miss her."

They switched to more usual topics for a first date: music, movies and TV shows, books, sports, what they liked to do in their spare time. Kind of pointless, she kept thinking, given that she had no intention of staying in Leclaire and was, in fact, half wishing she hadn't come at all.

Except, if she hadn't, she wouldn't have met Jack. And wasn't that an unnerving thought. She couldn't remember ever being so conscious of a man—every shift of expression, his big hands, his crooked smile and that undisciplined hair.

He'd handed over his credit card to the waiter when she heard herself say, "So, this guy who tried to break into Ric's house. What do you think that was about?" Apparently, her subconscious had been dwelling on the near break-in.

Looking surprised, Jack said, "Probably the usual. Every place is plagued with that kind of crap. We have drugs, gangs and stupid teenagers here, too."

"You don't think—" Her throat seemed to close up.

"That it had anything to do with your mother? How could it?"

She stiffened at what sounded like condescension, but couldn't really blame him. "Never mind," she mumbled.

His forehead creased. "Or are you thinking someone is reacting to you coming home?"

"Of course not!"

"You saw it happen, didn't you?"

Had he just dredged that up out of his memory? Gabby wanted to think so. Either way, she didn't like his next question.

"There's no reason you'd be a threat to anyone, is there?"

SHE REACTED TO his question as if he'd just accused her of child abuse. Her eyes widened in either shock or outrage and she snapped, "Of course not! In case you don't know, I was a complete failure as a witness." Without looking at him again, she shoved back her chair and jumped to her feet.

The waiter who'd just brought Jack's card back and the slip for him to sign looked surprised.

Jack scribbled his autograph and pocketed his credit card without even pulling out his wallet. Gabby quivered as if she wanted to run away, but she waited for him to stand and walk her to the coat rack at the entrance.

Once they'd bundled up and left the restaurant, he said quietly, "I'm sorry. I get used to asking nosy questions. I didn't mean to upset you."

"I'm not upset." She walked fast, keeping a distance between them on the sidewalk.

He'd had to park farther away tonight; he could just as well have walked her back to the hotel, but he was glad she hadn't turned that way. They'd have had no privacy at all. She sure as hell wasn't going to invite him up to her room.

Once at the hotel, he pulled into an Unload zone. "I really am sorry. I was having a good time."

"I was, too," she said softly.

"Okay." No sign of a valet or any pedestrians at the moment. He realized she was looking at him, her face a pale oval.

The temptation he'd felt since he set eyes on her overrode his common sense. Jack leaned forward and kissed her.

Chapter Four

Jack's warm mouth captured hers. This was no gentle good-night kiss. Oh, no. He ran his tongue down the seam of her lips until Gabby parted them. Then he nibbled at them, stroked her tongue, kneaded the nape of her neck with a big, strong hand. She succumbed with shocking speed, grabbing a fistful of his shirt-front to keep herself from sliding to the floorboards, and kissed him back.

When he lifted his head, they stared at each other. Passing headlights illuminated his face, highlighting every craggy feature, before darkness shadowed it. She'd never so much wanted to ask a man to share her bed even if it would be a one-night stand, but that wasn't something she ever did. And she couldn't forget the sting from his questions.

She opened her fingers to release his shirt, clenching her hands on her lap instead. "You think I'm a coward," she said in a voice huskier than her usual.

"Coward? What are you—" Comprehension brought him to a stop.

Gabby turned her head and gazed straight ahead

at the rear of another SUV parked at the curb in front of them. "Ric accuses me often enough. Maybe he's even right. I'd have more respect for his opinion if he had any idea what it was like. It would be bad enough as an adult to see that kind of violence happen right in front of you, but I was a little girl. I remember men who interviewed me back then assuming that I saw it like a cartoon. You know, the anvil drops on Road-runner, flattening him. But naturally, he squeaks out from under, shakes himself and, except for a lump on his head, all is well."

"Children do see enough cartoon violence to equate it to—"

She ignored him. "It was *nothing* like a cartoon. Nothing. I didn't for a second think she'd pop back up and start making sandwiches. Watching my mother die was horrible beyond belief. I'll bet even you've never seen anything like that."

"I see more than you'd think."

She shook her head. "The aftermath. And you didn't love the person whose body was lying right in front of you. She wasn't your mommy."

"No." Pure gravel, his voice shouldn't have been comforting, but was. "You're right."

"Do I want to remember every gory detail, even if I could after twenty-five years?" Wasn't that what she hoped to do? Still, she looked fiercely at him. "I would if I thought I could identify her killer. But I was so fixated on—" She pressed a hand to her mouth.

"Gabby." He reached over and gently took her

hand, pulling it away from her mouth, holding on to it in a warm grip. "You'll give yourself nightmares."

Her laughter burned her chest. "Oh, I have nightmares, no matter what I do. They never go away." She wrenched her hand from his, undid the seat belt clasp and reached for the door handle. "Thank you for dinner—"

"Please," he said. "If I promise not to raise the subject, can we have dinner again tomorrow night?"

"I already promised Ric." She climbed out onto the sidewalk. "I don't know if he'd be mad if you joined us… But that's not what you had in mind."

"I'll take what I can get," he said with what sounded like real honesty. "Lunch?"

Gabby hesitated. He knew she'd be leaving town within a few days if not weeks. Why was he pursuing her like this? He'd probably had a dozen girlfriends more beautiful than she was.

Did he like the idea of an end date? Get her in bed without having to worry about her getting clingy?

But something in his expression gave her pause. For whatever reason, however brief their acquaintance, she *mattered* to him. Even during dinner, she remembered the way he'd never looked away from her face. She wanted to dismiss the very idea, but couldn't quite, because from the minute she saw him walking toward her through the Italian restaurant, she'd reacted to him in a completely unfamiliar way. He might be as confounded as she was.

That wasn't impossible, was it?

"Can you really get away for lunch?"

"Sure I can." There was the cocky guy she'd first met. "*And* dinner."

Gabby had to laugh. "Ric and I are going back to that same Italian restaurant," she said. "We've resolved to try something besides pizza. Supposedly, the food is great. Um. He said he'd made reservations for six thirty."

"It is great. That's why I picked it in the first place." Jack's mouth curved. "Shall I surprise him?"

"How about if we have lunch, and then talk about it?"

"Deal." He suggested calling her in the morning to set a time to pick her up.

Gabby agreed, shivered and realized how cold she was, and slammed the car door. She could see enough reflection in the double glass doors of the hotel to know Jack didn't pull away from the curb until she was safely inside.

JACK DROVE HOME in a crappy mood. Seeing the anguish Gabby had lived with for most of her life made him feel guilty as hell. She was right; as a cop, he'd seen countless gory, senseless scenes, picked up bodies off the pavement and pried them out of crushed metal in car accidents, studied multiple fatalities after someone had lost it or a family fractured into violence. But those were the bodies of strangers, not his loved ones, not even friends. He'd heard of cops called to a scene only to discover one of the fatalities was a daughter or wife. He'd have said he couldn't think of anything worse, but turns out there *was* a worse.

Watching the most important person in your world killed right in front of you.

He'd been bitter for years because she'd chosen not to relive that memory. Now he found out she did, whether she liked it or not, in the form of nightmares.

That kiss had hit him hard. If he'd had any intention, it was a peck on the lips—a first date, sitting in front of the hotel with a bellhop watching. That kind of kiss. But no. Stupidly, he'd surrendered to his intense attraction to this woman he was betraying every minute they spent together.

She would hate his guts when she found out that what he really wanted was to pick through her brain for clues, no matter what the experience did to her.

Yeah, but he was starting to want something else altogether, and he didn't like it. Mixed emotions were a bitch. He was used to setting goals and going for what he wanted. From the beginning, he'd understood that there might be some collateral damage, but his goals were important enough to justify it. He considered himself a decent man, but he enforced the law. He hunted for pieces of scum and brought them in even if he left a wife and little kids sobbing in his wake.

God, please don't let Gabby cry.

Let her hate him instead.

Once home, he locked up behind himself, gulped some milk from the carton in the refrigerator and turned off lights on his way upstairs to the bedroom.

He thought of the start he'd already made today in reviewing the crime. He could quit right now. Tell his sergeant and Chief Keller that she didn't remember anything useful. She'd been too young to be any kind of witness. They'd buy it.

In the bathroom, Jack stared at himself in the mirror over the sink. He could do that—if he could let go of the goal that had driven half the choices he'd made in his life. If he could look his father in the eye the next time he saw him, knowing he'd thrown away the chance to clear Dad's name, once and for all, allowing him to straighten his shoulders when he faced the world...

And then there was the fact that he now knew Gabby still had nightmares about her mother's murder—and what were those nightmares but memories waiting to be brought out of the dark?

Jack tore his gaze from his own face, groaned and scraped a hand over the stubble on his jaw.

Yeah, it was self-serving to think that what he'd also be doing was stealing from Gabby the chance to make her own awful memories really mean something. They haunted her; she'd acknowledged as much. If he could help her remember her mother's killer, wouldn't that free Gabby, too? She might not see it that way right now, but she would eventually.

Even if she also ended up hating his guts.

He grimaced. Something told him he wouldn't be sleeping like a baby tonight.

WITH REGRET, JACK left Gabby in the lobby of her hotel in front of the elevators. Conversation had ranged widely while they ate lunch at a deli a few blocks down the street. As he'd promised, it never touched on her mother, brother or early years here in Leclaire. Jack discovered her viewpoints were liberal and well defended. She did concede that, given his job, he had reason to look at the world with a more jaundiced viewpoint. She made him laugh more often than he had in recent memory, even as his gut stayed tight from guilt.

He had kissed her lightly before they parted because he couldn't not. He wanted to join her and her brother for dinner, but had a bad feeling that his hunger to see her this evening, too, didn't have anything to do with his cold case investigation.

Walking out to his SUV, he was glad the hotel had had the parking lot plowed. Yeah, snow had fallen last night, and tiny flakes still floated down. Pretty, but a pain in the butt for patrol officers who'd be responsible for endless fender benders, getting pickup trucks pulled out of ditches, and nailing idiots who wouldn't slow down on icy roads.

He interviewed the contractor who had reported the theft of the construction equipment, not going so far as to make accusations, but persistent enough the guy was getting rattled by the time Jack thanked him for his time and left. Sure as hell, he'd sold the bulldozer, forklift and all the rest, and now expected to double his profit with an insurance payoff. Some digging had uncovered the fact that the contractor had never gotten out of debt after selling the last houses he'd built. Now he was in real trouble. This little scheme would allow him to pay the bills for another month or so, maybe long enough to finish the current building and sell it. Harmless, he'd think...except the insurance company wouldn't agree.

Minor corruption might end the guy's career.

Back at the station, Jack made more phone calls and did more computer research about other cases. He had roughly fifteen active cases and a dozen or more he kept at the back of his mind. And now he'd added a cold case. There was plenty to keep him busy, and no excuse for him to resent not being able to concentrate 100 percent on that cold case—or to be letting his mind wander to Gabby Ortiz and the way his heart stumbled when she smiled at him.

Brooding about her evening plans, he wrestled with himself, finally concluding that she and her brother needed time together without him there as a diversion. He'd call her in the morning.

Damn, he hadn't grocery shopped in a week. He wasn't in the mood to cook anyway. Maybe he'd go through a drive-through...

Or maybe he should concentrate on doing his job.

GABBY COULDN'T BELIEVE she hadn't packed any extra elastics for her hair. Since breaking her only one, she'd had to leave her hair out of its normal braid. Fortunately, there was no wind today as she walked the three blocks to the pharmacy the concierge had suggested. She declined his offer to summon an Uber. A walk sounded good.

The bitter cold made her feel right at home, as did the crunching sound underfoot from either salt that had been spread on the sidewalk or refrozen slush thrown from car tires or left by the plow. A New Englander, she was used to seeing her own breath in white plumes, and just walking briskly was a pleasure. She'd spent too much of her brief stay in Leclaire in her hotel room, a restaurant or one car or another.

At the pharmacy, she grabbed a package of hair elastics in multicolors and several other toiletries, just in case. She stumbled on a surprisingly sizeable book and magazine section, too, and chose a couple of books. After paying, she stepped back out onto the sidewalk, deiced here by a generous application of salt.

The green walk signal at the corner flashed. Since walking in the bitter cold was one thing but standing around another, she hustled to make it. One glance told her no cars were waiting on the cross street at the intersection. An approaching SUV had plenty of time to stop. These must be the old-fashioned lights that changed at regular interludes no matter what traffic was doing.

Her mind started to wander. Even though she had good reason for wariness where Jack was concerned, she wished that they'd set another time to get together—and that his goodbye kiss had been more than a peck.

She was shocked back to the present by the huge SUV racing toward her at an unsafe speed. No sign the driver was braking for the light. Oh, damn, her walk signal had turned red while she'd been distracted. The driver must see her, surely, but Gabby broke into a jog anyway.

Her foot caught a bit of ice and she slipped, staggering to keep her feet. The SUV hadn't slowed at all, and suddenly assumed monstrous proportions. On a burst of adrenaline, Gabby dove forward toward the sanctuary of a parked car. One of her feet scraped against the black metal.

And then she hit the hard, icy pavement and skidded until her head bumped the curb.

Winded and shocked, it took her a minute to realize the speeding vehicle had gone through the intersection and continued on straight ahead, the driver apparently oblivious to the pedestrian he—or she—had just about taken out.

She heard running footsteps. Voices called out, blending together. "Are you all right?"

"Did you fall?"

Only one said, "Man, I wish I'd gotten the license plate."

Gabby struggled to sit. A couple of the people who'd reached her stepped forward to help her up. She winced when she put weight on her right foot, but she was sure it wasn't broken. Someone else retrieved her shopping bag, which had gone flying. Fortunately, it was intact.

The anxious, kind faces around her were the reassurance she needed to smile. "Thanks. To all of you. Um…did any of you see the license plate of that SUV? Or even notice what make or model it was?"

Most people had been half a block or more away

and hadn't. A few hadn't noticed a vehicle at all. The two people who'd been closest agreed it was black, but argued about whether it had been a Chevy or a Dodge or...

She gave up, decided her ankle would support her, and hobbled the two more blocks she had to go.

Hotel staff rushed to her in alarm, but she assured them she'd taken a tumble but was fine. All she needed was a hot shower. Thanks to her heavy garments and gloves, the only place she'd even skinned a little was her jaw, and she had antibiotic ointment in her travel first aid kit.

A bellboy insisted on walking her up to her room and refused a tip.

Gabby sank onto her bed, a lot shakier than she'd let any of the strangers see. She had come within inches of being badly injured or even killed.

Of course it was an accident. It had to be. Maybe the sun had been in the driver's eyes, or he'd been distracted by an incoming text. After all, who *hadn't* ever been distracted while behind the wheel?

It was just... She closed her eyes. One of the "incidents" that had preceded Great-Aunt Isabel taking her away had been another near miss. That time, she'd been on her training bike on the sidewalk. Just sitting there. She'd been outside only because Dad had insisted she do something besides watch TV or cling to him.

It was a sedan that time. She hadn't been paying attention at all, but Mr. Monroe next door saw it jump the curb. He'd come out for his mail, and snatched her out of the way barely in time. The car flattened her bike, swerved back onto the street and burned rubber as it ran the stop sign on the next corner and kept going.

The driver was probably a drunk or a reckless teenager who'd gotten the scare of his life, people kept saying. Even the police didn't take it all that seriously. Dad did. Only a week before, a bullet had hit the fender of his car in the grocery store parking lot, missing her by inches. Drive-by shootings had been a recent problem, the responding officer had told him gravely. But only days later, Dad found a plastic container of cookies on their doorstep with a note that said, "In sympathy." Neighbors always rang the doorbell, they didn't leave anonymous gifts. He was suspicious enough to take those cookies to the police, who determined they contained rat poison. While the cookies could have harmed Dad or Ric, too, she was the smallest and would have likely been killed.

Today was different, she promised herself. Even if she'd been hit, she was more likely to have been injured than killed. Unless she'd been flung ahead of the SUV and the driver had just gone right over her and still fled. One of her most powerful flickers of childhood memory was seeing her beloved bike— pink, of course—crushed on the sidewalk. Could a human body look like that?

No. Ridiculous.

Gabby blew out a long breath and decided she should call Jack anyway.

SHE TALKED HIM out of racing to her side, but it was a close call. Jack knew he couldn't actually do anything, and had a suspicion she'd downplay any after-effects of the near miss. She was seeing her brother tonight, though, and it would be hard to hide any injuries from him.

Jack had grilled her about every detail of what happened. He couldn't believe she hadn't gotten the names and phone numbers of any of the witnesses.

"But they didn't see anything!" she kept protesting.

Except for the two of them who agreed with her that the vehicle had been a full-size SUV, and black. And one, she admitted, had been sure the driver was a man. "Big," he said, and maybe wearing a baseball cap.

Jack made some calls to find out whether any nearby stores had security cameras, or whether that intersection had a traffic camera. The answer was no. The city of Leclaire was running behind on updating old traffic lights and adding camera surveillance that would reveal the license plates of vehicles that ran a red light. The first was just a money issue, while the cameras faced significant protest among residents rebelling at the idea of being watched.

What if Gabby had died today and they couldn't arrest the hit-and-run driver in part because of the lack of new technology? Jack ground his teeth.

"Cowan?"

He spun his desk chair to face Sergeant Rutkowski.

"There a problem?" the sergeant asked, no doubt registering his expression.

"Gabrielle Ortiz was damn close to being the victim of a hit-and-run accident this afternoon. She had to dive out of the way of a speeding vehicle."

The sergeant's homely face creased. "By her brother's house?"

"No, she was downtown doing some errands. She'd just left the Walgreens and was crossing a street. Unfortunately, there were no witnesses close enough to catch a license plate, and none of them even agreed on the make or model of the vehicle. I can't find a camera in the vicinity. It's a dead end."

Rutkowski frowned down at him. "You don't think this was a deliberate attack."

Jack took a few deep breaths before he answered. "It's unlikely. I can't rule it out, though, because there were several possible attempts on her life right after her mother's murder. One could have been malicious, although investigators couldn't figure out a motive. The other incidents could fall into the bad luck category, but all these things happened in a matter of weeks."

The echo of the speeding vehicle and a driver who didn't stop sent up a flare for him now that he couldn't ignore.

"Have you read up on the Ortiz murder?" he asked.

"I did when I first came on board with this unit," the sergeant said, "but it's been years."

Unsurprised, Jack said, "One of those three near misses was a car jumping the curb by her house. She'd be dead if a neighbor hadn't been close enough to snatch her out of the way. Car swerved back onto the street and booked it. Investigators didn't find any-thing."

"I don't blame you for being uneasy," Rutkowski said, "but unless a better witness comes forward…" He shrugged.

Jack's jaw ached as he watched the sergeant walk away. No, there wasn't a damn thing he could do, and he didn't like it.

He accomplished some more work, but still felt unsettled when he left the station earlier than usual. Maybe he'd go to the gym. Some hard exercise might reduce his tension. Between the weather and Gabby, he hadn't gotten in a workout in nearly a week.

He was still waiting for his car to warm up when his phone rang. He groaned. He should be down the list to have to take the next crime referred to the unit…but someone ahead of him could be sick, snowed in, who knew. Only then he got the phone out of his pocket. Ric again? Jack accepted the call and put it on speaker.

This couldn't be good news.

Chapter Five

Fifteen minutes later, Jack parked at the curb in front of Ric's house. Walking up the driveway, he scanned the facade. Gabby was right; he might have time traveled. Not one single thing about the exterior of this house had changed from the days when this had been a frequent stop on the carpool circuit.

A patrol officer walked out the front door and saw him. They met a few steps from the porch.

"Could just be teenagers," Officer Engman said, but not sounding as if he believed it. "Strange after the attempted break-in night before last, though."

Jack knew Engman, although not well. "Has there been an upsurge of this kind of thing in the neighborhood?"

"No." A few years younger than Jack but no rookie, Engman gazed at the house. "This area is one of the safest in town. Mostly homeowners—people know each other." He shrugged. "We patrol here, but not as often as we do around Hawthorn or west Leclaire."

Jack nodded his understanding. "Mr. Ortiz inside?"

"Yeah. Not happy."

Jack grunted. "You'll write a report?"

"Yes, and recommend we drive by more often, at least for a few days."

"Good. Thanks."

Engman left. Ric met Jack at the door.

"Had to be the same guy," he growled.

Jack hadn't liked the coincidence of the original attempted break-in coupled with rumors spreading about Gabby's return to Leclaire. That somebody would take the chance to come back to the same house, break a window and let himself in, this time in broad daylight? And, oh yeah, while leaving a trampled path in the snow around the side of the house? Of course it was the same guy, with the same goal.

"Anything stolen?" he asked.

"Yeah, smaller electronics. A brand-new iPad, a nice pair of wireless earphones and a portable keyboard. I'm out maybe a couple of thousand dollars."

"That could have been the point," Jack felt he had to say.

"You kidding me?"

"No, I don't believe it any more than you do." He nodded past Ric. "You going to let me in?"

"Yeah. Sorry."

"Did Gabby tell you what happened this afternoon?"

"Shit. Yeah. I got to tell you, I don't like any of this."

Jack didn't either, even if it was hard to imagine somebody had broken in here, searched the house, then happened to get lucky enough to not only spot her, but be in a position to take a run at her when she crossed a side street alone.

They started a walk-through, which didn't tell him much except that the kitchen looked exactly like it had in the twenty-five-year-old crime scene photos he'd pored over. Jack was with Gabby on this one; how had her father, and now Ric, been able to stay in this place?

The door to the garage, which had only one of those useless push-button locks, had been unlocked when Ric got home. To get to it, they passed through the utility room. He hated seeing how close the long-ago killer had been to Gabby's hiding place when he'd walked out.

The garage was remarkably tidy, Jack saw, a home to tools, lawn mower and presumably Ric's car, but not much else. A few tubs sat on shelves, but they were all made of clear plastic, revealing obvious stuff like Christmas decorations.

"Don't you have boxes of old family pictures, record albums, stamp collections and, I don't know, your parents' stuff that you don't know what to do with?" he asked.

Ric looked surprised. "Uh, yeah. In a small storage unit. Dad started it and… I've just kept paying for it." He sounded chagrined. "I know that's dumb when there's so much room here, but… Dad wanted it out of the house."

Dad, Jack couldn't help thinking, had some major issues that included denial.

Ric's brow creased. "Maybe Gabby and I could go through it."

There was a concept. Not that Jack didn't suspect he'd find an accumulation of crap at his dad's current house, when the time came.

Back in the house, Jack asked, "Was everything that was stolen out in plain sight?"

"Yeah." They'd mounted the stairs, and Ric led the way into what was apparently his bedroom. "And everything taken was downstairs. Have a look at this," he said, pulling open the drawer in the bedside stand.

Jack looked down at the watch that lay atop some clutter. Stainless steel, but the name on it was Longines, which he had a feeling meant expensive.

"That's a two-thousand-dollar watch," Ric said flatly. "Perfect condition."

"So either this guy didn't bother opening drawers, or he didn't know the watch was worth anything." Which argued teenager or a druggie, but Jack didn't bother saying so. He thought a few pieces of electronics had been grabbed as a cover.

"Closet doors are open, but nothing's been touched. Same for the master bath. He did check out both of the spare bedrooms, which are obviously unoccupied." Ric stood aside to let Jack walk into the first room, where one side of the standard double-closet doors had been pushed open. Ditto in the second, across the hall. In both rooms, the closets were empty, no boxed-up miscellany there.

Both rooms seemed impersonal; if the downstairs had gone unchanged, that wasn't the case up here.

Neither bedroom shouted "teenage boy," although the walls in one room were painted pink. Left that way in case Gabby ever came home? At some point, Ric had moved into the master bedroom, which either he or his father had thoroughly updated.

Jack looked into the hall bathroom and saw that the medicine cabinet door was open a crack and one drawer on the vanity had been dropped on the floor.

"He wanted to know whether you had a house-guest," Jack said slowly.

"That's my take." Ric looked grim. "Now he knows I don't."

The two men stared at each other.

"This is crazy thinking," Jack said after a minute. "She testified at the time. Why would she be a threat to him?"

"I don't know. He's afraid she saw his face?"

"So what if she did? She was four years old. If she'd recognized the man, she'd have said so then. Now what can she say? He had brown eyes and he looked mad?"

Ric shoved his fingers through his hair. "Do I tell her?"

Crap. Jack thought fast. Did he have to admit that he'd already reopened the investigation into Colleen Ortiz's murder? Ric would be glad he had, in one way, but he'd also immediately understand how Jack had used him.

And then there was Gabby.

His instinct still said to put it off. Be a friend, not

an investigator. Jack could see her clamming up right away. But…

Reluctant, he said, "I think we have to. She needs to be careful."

"What if she just decides to leave town?" Ric sounded frustrated and helpless, both feelings Jack shared.

He tried to be honest with himself. Would she be safer if she did go? Or now that she'd appeared and possibly scared the killer, would he figure it was worth the cost of a round-trip airline ticket to shut her up permanently?

"I'd rather she stay where we can keep an eye on her," he said at last. "But she may not see it that way."

Ric suddenly swore. "What time is it?"

"Ah…" Jack checked his phone. "Just after six."

"I'm supposed to meet her for dinner. I've got to go."

Jack swallowed what he really wanted to say. "Have you boarded over the broken window?"

"Why bother, when the horse is long gone?" Ric grimaced. "No, but I can do it quick. I have some lumber scraps in the garage."

Jack waited in the kitchen while Gabby's brother disappeared into the garage. The kitchen door had a glass pane, something that was all but an invitation to robbers, in Jack's opinion. The dead bolt lock would be useless.

Not that he could say much, given that he'd replaced the original French doors at his place with ones that still suited the age of the house but were double-paned. Security-wise, they weren't a good choice, though.

Once Ric had positioned a small piece of plywood over the broken window, Jack handed over nails for Ric to tap in.

"Might want to consider replacing this door," he suggested mildly. "Steel might be good, no glass."

"That has crossed my mind." Ric cleaned up and they went through the house to the front door. "Listen, I don't know if you have plans. If not, you're welcome to join us for dinner."

"If you're sure, I'd like that." He hoped his eagerness wasn't too apparent. "She told me you're going back to the same place."

"Yeah, I'm picking her up." Ric pulled out a key fob and unlocked his car. "See you there?"

"I'll be right behind you."

Ric was already backing out of the driveway when Jack got into his own vehicle. He started it up, but didn't touch the gearshift right away. Instead, he studied the house, trapped in a time warp. He agreed wholeheartedly with Gabby.

It was creepy.

And he had to wonder what Ric was thinking— and why it hadn't occurred to him how his little sister would feel about it. This being the little sister who'd actually *seen* her mother slaughtered, right there in the kitchen that appeared unchanged from that day to this one.

"But...it's RIDICULOUS to think someone breaking into your house has anything to do with me!" Gabby exclaimed. She suppressed the flicker of fear but not that anxiety that had flared when she heard how the house had been searched.

She and the two men claimed the same booth at the restaurant, except this time Jack had achieved what she guessed was his preference for having his back to the wall. He'd slid into that seat fast enough, and she'd seen the way he scanned the restaurant before he grimly studied the abrasion on her jaw. Even now, his gaze kept flicking from her eyes to that scrape.

"Did Jack put this into your head?" she demanded of her brother, sitting beside her. "I can understand why *he'd* be paranoid."

"Gee, thanks," Jack said, with a hint of amusement.

Ric glared at her. "Because I'm so easily influenced?"

"Well…you know what I mean."

"I do, and no. I'd have had to be an idiot not to realize that whoever searched the house was more interested in the guest bedrooms and bath than he was in my room or downstairs. Yeah, he picked up a few small electronics that can be sold, but he'd have found more if he'd looked. What could he have imagined would be stowed in the hall bathroom?"

"Prescription drugs?"

"In a bathroom I obviously don't use?" Her brother shook his head. "I hate to say it, but I'm glad you didn't agree to stay with me."

The anxiety was growing. Gabby nibbled on her lower lip. "Who even knows I'm in town?"

Ric gave her a list that kept growing. "I thought

people who remembered you would be glad to know you're visiting."

He sounded defensive, she couldn't help noticing.

She turned her gaze to Jack, a solid presence she'd have thought to be reassuring if it weren't for the way he watched her. Assessing her reaction, she guessed. To see if she was faking it?

She'd already had a really crappy day and more aches and pains than she'd expected. She didn't need this.

Suddenly mad, she said, "Mom was killed twenty-five years ago. I was four. Four years old!"

"Almost five," Jack murmured.

"Do *you* remember much from the year before you started kindergarten?"

"A few things that made an impression."

"Like?"

His eyebrows rose at her challenge. "I saw big kids jumping from swings at the playground and decided to try it. Came down hard on my back. I vividly remember that moment, lying there, looking up at the sky, not able to breathe, pain just starting to roll over me."

Silenced, she didn't say anything.

"There was another time. Dad had taken us sledding. On the way back, a deer ran in front of the car. He had to slam on the brakes and we spun in a full circle before coming to a stop. It stunned me."

Gabby closed her eyes. He had made his point. Yes, she could summon the scene when her mother was stabbed, but—

"I think I closed my eyes some of the time," she mumbled. "I remember whimpering and then being so scared *he'd* hear me."

Jack reached his hand across the table, and she laid hers in that now-familiar, reassuring clasp, uncaring what Ric would think.

"It…none of it made sense to me. An adult might have been thinking, *I have to notice details so the police can catch him.* But I just tried not to move and hoped it would be over before I got so scared I had to run, because I knew he could catch me."

Jack gently loosened her hand and she saw that her fingernails had bitten into his flesh.

She also realized she'd hunched into herself as if she was a little girl again—squeezed into the corner, rounded her shoulders, pressed her knees together. She hadn't quite pulled her feet up to the seat so she could wrap herself into an even tinier ball, but it was close.

She hated that. It hadn't happened in a long time. Gabby swallowed and looked from Jack's face to her brother's and back again. She didn't like their expressions. She hadn't been asking for her brother's pity—or for Jack's unnerving, narrow-eyed interest.

It took some effort, but she loosened her body, lifted her chin and snatched her hand back from his grip. "You know, several police officers had me tell them what I saw. Enough that I started getting muddled." Now she glared at Ric, whose oft-expressed anger and contempt at her failure to point a finger at the killer had hurt her. Undermined her self-esteem, she had realized in recent years.

"Maybe I should take out an ad in the *Courier*? 'Child Witness No Help to Police.' How does that sound?"

Jack was either frowning or…bothered. "I half wish we could."

"Oh, for Pete's sake!" She looked down to see that she'd barely touched her salad, and a beaming waitress had arrived with their entrées. With a churning stomach, Gabby wasn't sure she could do any more justice to her bean ragout than she'd done to the salad.

Both men picked up their forks the minute the waitress walked away. *Their* appetites were apparently intact. Somehow, she wasn't surprised that Jack had ordered a more traditional entrée, lasagna alla Bolognese. Ric always had been an adventurer where food went. He'd ordered a pasta with mushrooms and white truffle oil.

With a sigh, she picked up her fork, too.

"Maybe we are being paranoid," Jack said suddenly. "I'll check out the hotel's security measures. We just want you to be careful. Be sure not to get caught alone. And be wary if someone you might or might not remember pops up, excited to see you again."

"What am I supposed to do? Sit in my room all day? Watch soaps?" Although at the moment she wasn't all that enthusiastic about going out on her own.

He flashed that infuriatingly sexy grin. "How about working on your dissertation?"

That *really* silenced her.

JACK PARTED RELUCTANTLY from Gabby and her brother out front of the restaurant. He trusted Ric to see her safely to her room, especially since he'd seized the opportunity when she went to the restroom to suggest Ric do a quick walk-through that included her bathroom.

He'd given a short laugh. "Peek behind the shower curtain, you mean? Bet she'll love that."

"Tell her you'll feel better."

"I will."

So would Jack, but he didn't say that. He hadn't kissed Gabby good-night, either, even lightly. Best not to introduce any more awkwardness between the three of them. Ric hadn't looked thrilled when Jack and Gabby had held hands. He wanted Ric to keep calling him with any worries or other strange events. And Gabby…he'd call her first thing tomorrow. Maybe from downstairs in the hotel he fully intended to assess for security weaknesses.

Noticing that the snow had stopped falling but wouldn't melt unless the temperature decided to rise tomorrow, Jack finally drove home. That was a word he used automatically, but despite the pleasure he'd taken in remodeling the house, he hadn't done much with furniture or decor. He still ate at the breakfast bar in the kitchen, leaving the dining area empty. Art was nonexistent. A few family pictures hung on the wall in the office. Those pictures motivated him. Every time he glanced at them, he could see what he'd have had if Colleen Ortiz hadn't been murdered—

and if the police hadn't failed to identify and arrest the killer.

The sight of those happy family moments used to work better. As an adult, he'd become cynical enough to suspect that whatever love—for want of a better word—had cemented his parents hadn't been very strong. He hadn't understood then, and still didn't, why his mother hadn't believed in his father. Why she'd let whispers influence her to doubt his fidelity and, worse, come to believe he was capable of committing a crime so brutal.

All in the absence of any actual facts beyond him having been seen knocking on the door at the Ortiz house the day before the murder.

The police believed Dad's explanation. Mom didn't.

After everything went down, Jack's father had been closemouthed about his mother, however broken he was when she left him not long after. He wouldn't criticize her, which Jack respected.

In the past few years, his cynicism deepened. Had Dad cheated on Mom at some point in the past? Was that why her trust had been so shaky?

Jack had trouble seeing it, though, and the possibility still didn't shake his belief in his father. Anyway, why wouldn't Mom have told him, once he was an adult? But she wouldn't defend herself; she just got mulish and pouty when he tried to get her to talk to him.

It had been several years since he'd bothered calling her at all. He talked a little more often with his sister, and regretted not getting to know her kids. But once Humpty Dumpty fell off the wall, there was no putting the pieces back together again.

Prowling through the house, he thought back to the day. Had somebody tried to kill Gabby, or was it pure happenstance she'd been in the way of a drunken or foolish driver? And then there was the break-in at the Ortiz house.

What surprised him was to discover that exhilaration had him feeling wired.

Gabby was opening up, whether she knew it or not. Twice now, she'd revealed memories so vivid, she'd reverted physically in small ways to the child she'd been. Over time, people's memories tended to blur; sometimes they altered. Who wanted to remember being a victim? It was better to convince yourself you'd really been heroic, or at least smart. She *was* smart to hide—but he doubted she'd think of it that way. If he'd sat down with Gabby in an interview room and insisted she tell him what she remembered, the narrative she offered wouldn't have convinced him. When she was flung back to *being* that child, he could almost see through her eyes.

Her small flashback tonight fully justified his somewhat underhanded tactics. If he'd taken the straightforward route, he'd have gotten nowhere.

The entire reel, beginning to end, was in Gabby Ortiz's head. If he could coax her into playing it, he'd finally catch the son of a bitch who'd killed her mother. He had closed a lot of cases since he became a detective, but this one would mean the most.

It was personal.

Chapter Six

The hot tub had felt fabulous this afternoon, but, sad to say, the therapeutic effect had worn off. A dip in the pool would feel good now.

On the other hand, Ric and Jack had combined to awaken uneasiness that made Gabby decide to wait until Jack—how had he put it?—assessed hotel security. If there weren't cameras in the pool area, she could be really isolated in the evening once families with children returned to their rooms.

And what if she wasn't alone? A guy on his own might wander in. If he was young enough, she wouldn't have to worry, but what if he was in his forties, say? Fifties? She wouldn't recognize anyone her parents had once known.

She'd already had an eventful day and didn't need to add any more stress. Digging out the ibuprofen she carried in her handbag, she took two with water. She could brew a cup of coffee, but that seemed like too much effort. She grabbed the two books she'd bought today, determined to start one of them. Worry was clearly going to make it hard to concentrate, though.

Now that she'd gotten together with Ric a few times, maybe she should give up and go home. Except, the apartment in Concord she'd probably be giving up soon wasn't home, and she'd sold Aunt Isabel's house to pay off student loans as well as grad school tuition.

Face it—she didn't have anything approaching a true home. Which was probably the most deep-seated reason, she admitted ruefully to herself, she was here in Leclaire. It had called to her. It was once home, and Ric was her only family. He even lived in the family home.

Too bad she wished that it had burned down to the foundation at some point in the past twenty-five years.

Knowing she'd really lost it at dinner humiliated her. Would Jack bother to call again after seeing her childish display?

Sure he would, Gabby thought, depressed; he'd promised to do that security check, and he would. He'd feel obligated to report on it, too. To offer further advice, probably.

And if he didn't suggest dinner or lunch...well, she should be glad. No, Leclaire didn't feel like home, either, and she wouldn't be staying. Why start something with a guy she'd never see again once she left town?

Knock, knock.

She jerked. A quick glance toward the digital alarm clock on the bedside table told her it was 9:05. Who could possibly be here?

For some reason, she tiptoed to the door. Thank

goodness she'd not only locked it, she'd put on that latch doohickey, too. "Who is it?" she called.

"Room service, ma'am." The voice was a man's.

"I didn't order anything."

She couldn't entirely make out what he said, but the word *complimentary* was in there. That wasn't impossible. This was a classy hotel. She actually reached for the knob before she thought better of it.

You need to be sure not to get caught alone.

There might be security cameras in the hallways, but there wouldn't be in the rooms. There'd better not be, anyway.

"Thank you, but I don't want anything," she called back. "I'll let room service know I refused you."

Then she listened hard.

The man didn't say anything. No *Very well, ma'am*.

She didn't hear footsteps, either, although with the plush carpet in the hall, she probably wouldn't. But if he'd knocked on any neighboring doors, she'd probably hear that, if only faintly. And if she was being offered some complimentary goodies, wouldn't you think other people staying here would be, too?

Nothing. The hush was so complete, it scared her even more.

She backed away from the door. Hurried to the slider that led out to a balcony and checked that lock, too.

Then, heart pounding, she sat back down. She was okay. The waiter was probably legit—but she'd tell Jack about him.

GALVANIZED, JACK TURNED back to the security office even before he ended the midmorning call to Gabby. He didn't fool himself that it could be this easy. He had too much experience watching endless security footage, only to find it too grainy to make out the needed detail, or to learn that the camera pointed the wrong way. His favorite was being told that a particular camera hadn't been operative for weeks or months. Business owners invariably thought that the existence of a visible camera was good enough.

The head of security answered the knock on the door, looking startled at Jack's quick reappearance. At least he'd taken Jack seriously, especially after being told that one of the hotel guests had come damn close yesterday to being killed on an icy street only two blocks away.

"You have another question?"

"I just spoke to the woman in question." He explained about the knock on her door after nine last night, and that the man knocking had claimed to be a waiter with something complimentary for her.

Art Lessiter shook his head immediately. "Truffles are placed in every room daily by cleaning staff. Occasionally we offer something like a free spa service to make up for an unsatisfactory experience here at the Wilmont, but we would never send food that hasn't been ordered." He sounded deadly serious. "And to expect a single woman guest to open her door to a male staff member, when she hadn't requested food or assistance? Aside from common sense, that could open us—and rightly so—to liability. I feel confident in saying that whoever knocked on her door is not employed by this hotel."

Nothing Lessiter said was a surprise to Jack. "Let's see the footage. She said the knock came at 9:05, although she was looking at the bedside clock, not her phone. Those wouldn't be as accurate."

"The maid is supposed to check the time on the clocks daily."

Jack waited tensely. He could see the current view of some hallways on screens. None of those were watched 24-7; whoever was on shift switched between cameras regularly.

It took Lessiter a minute, but once told the room number, he found what they were looking for. "I'm starting it at 8:55. We can go back further if we have to."

Both men stared at the monitor displaying a currently empty hallway in black-and-white—really an overall gray. One minute in, the elevator doors slid open and a couple emerged, turning toward the camera. They were smiling as they let themselves into a room.

A single man in a business suit came out of the elevator next, expression preoccupied, and walked away, passing Gabby's room and letting himself in to one several doors down and across the hall.

Then nothing.

At 9:04, the elevator opened and another man emerged. He was well dressed in a suit and overcoat, had on gloves that were probably leather, and wore a black fedora that hid his face. He started down the hall without once exposing his face to the camera.

Jack stored up his impressions. This guy was good-sized, bulky in a way that suggested a once-athletic man who had softened. He had a slightly rolling gait. And damn, he stopped outside Gabby's door and knocked.

He also kept his back turned to the camera. Presumably he spoke, because he waited for a minute. Then he strode away—in the other direction.

"Is there another elevator?"

"Yes, around the corner."

The security chief found that footage. The man reappeared on it, but only briefly to open a door that Lessiter said was to the staircase.

This footage was from a camera on the fourth floor looking down. Gabby's room was on the third floor, so they could see only the set of the shoulders and the top of the fedora.

He continued down to the garage and immediately let himself out a steel door that led to the alley at the back of the hotel.

And that was it.

But Lessiter went back to the camera footage taken in the stairwell. Inched it forward, then froze it. "Tell me I'm imagining that."

Jack leaned forward and cursed. Something black filled the space between the collar of the wool overcoat and the hat. "A balaclava," he said.

"Most people would think ski mask." The security chief sat back in his chair, his expression incredulous. "If he'd happened to meet someone getting out of the elevator, say, he could have pulled it down a little and mumbled something about not being used to nights this cold. Even without the hat, we wouldn't have seen his face."

He could not believe this. Colleen Ortiz's killer—or so the odds suggested—had been captured by three different cameras, and not one had revealed his features or anything else meaningful.

Except, that wasn't true. Yeah, the overcoat hid his body build, but not entirely. He was a good-sized man, tall and broad. He carried himself with shoulders squared—and then there was a distinctive gait.

"He knew where our cameras are," Lessiter said suddenly.

"He's either stayed here before and paid attention, or he cased the hotel. I wonder, if we went back…"

"When I have time, I might do just that." This was a pissed security chief.

"Let me know." Jack stood and thanked Art Lessiter, who promised to send copies of the footage to Jack.

Then Jack took the elevator himself, needing to see with his own eyes that Gabby was safe and well.

WHEN SHE ANSWERED the door, it was to find Jack wearing a suit, white shirt and tie. He looked extraordinarily handsome, but she surveyed him all the way down to his shiny black dress shoes with her eyebrows raised.

"I have to appear in court this afternoon," he said gruffly. "Don't get used to this."

A sharp pang served as a warning. She *wanted* to get used to Jack Cowan in all his manifestations—but it wasn't happening, she told herself.

Once Gabby agreed to have lunch with him, Jack said, "I'll be back in a couple of hours. Otherwise, unless you're having dinner with Ric tonight..." He paused meaningfully.

"What, I'm supposed to just skip meals?"

"You're not taking this seriously," he told her, his tone stern.

Maybe she had sounded a little sarcastic. "I am. I'm just not used to taking orders." She could be diplomatic when necessary, especially where academic politics were concerned, but obeying without question? No.

She'd spent a lifetime trying to insure she never felt helpless again. If that occasionally made her prickly, so be it.

The timbre of Jack's voice changed, became intimate. "You're right. I'm sorry. I'm used to snapping out orders and assuming people will jump to obey them. I just want you to be extra careful, okay?"

Gabby sighed. "I won't leave the hotel. Like I said, I'll leave the room only if I hear multiple people in the hall. It's just—" She hesitated.

"You don't want to order room service. I get that. *I* don't want you answering the door for anyone but me or Ric."

Left alone, Gabby plunked her laptop on the worktable and stared at it for a long time. Jack was right, this was a great block of time she could use to polish her dissertation. But there was no way she could really concentrate.

Great excuse, a voice seemed to whisper.

She ignored it. She changed back to her pajamas and spent the morning alternately reading and streaming shows she'd always wanted to catch up on. She even napped.

The firm knock on the door came at precisely noon. "It's me," Jack said, loud enough for her to hear.

She let him in before noticing he carried a laptop case under his arm. "I thought we were going out."

His sharp blue eyes stayed on her face. "We are, but I want to show you that footage first. In case this guy looks familiar to you."

"How could he?"

He'd think she was determined to bury her head in the sand, but realistically, how could she relate camera images to a man she'd seen once, when she was four years old?

Unless, of course, she should have known him because he'd been at the house before, like Jack's father had, or even more often if he'd been one of Mom and Dad's friends.

No matter what, she resented both Ric's *and* Jack's automatic assumption that she was a coward. She couldn't have denied that she carried the trauma that had shaped her life as if it was an unhealed wound, painful, hot, somewhere inside her chest, or that she'd spent much of her life refusing to examine it too closely. But she was trying to change that, and neither of the men knew how hard it was to do that. They had no idea how many times Aunt Isabel had insisted she had to put it behind her.

Jack had been watching her, as if he guessed she was fuming, but all he said, mildly, was "You've been out on your own a few times since you got into town, right? It's possible this guy has followed you."

Cold fingers slipped up her spine.

She retreated to the bed. "I thought you said you couldn't make out anything about his appearance."

Jack sat beside her, his greater weight compressing the mattress. She raised her head to meet his gaze and saw the tenderness on his face.

"The way people are built and move can be individual enough that we recognize someone coming from a distance away. Not everyone, but you know what I mean."

She did—and had the sinking feeling that Jack was one of those people for her. His long, athletic stride, the set of his shoulders, the way he so often turned his head as he remained aware of everyone and everything around him... Oh, yes, she'd know him long before she could see his face.

She only nodded.

He removed a thin laptop, opened it and called up an app and then the camera footage. Then he handed the computer to her and tapped a key to set the still picture into motion.

Gabby wasn't sure she breathed as she watched the elevator open and a man step out with his head bent and angled away from the camera. He walked down the hall. If he glanced at room numbers, she couldn't tell. He stopped at her door, raised a gloved hand and knocked.

Her lips moved as she mouthed what he'd said, what she'd said, and remembered the silence. Without physically showing any frustration, he walked swiftly away from the camera until he disappeared around a corner in the hall.

"You're shaking," Jack said with quick concern. He wrapped his arm around her, took the laptop away and set it on the bed, then cuddled her close. "I'm sorry. I wish—"

"I needed to see it," she mumbled against his shoulder.

"Was anything about him familiar?"

She shook her head vehemently, even though... she didn't know.

"There's something," he said slowly.

"Yes...no." She swallowed. "I don't know. It's just that seeing him makes it real. A stranger wanted me to let him into my room last night. It wasn't some kind of mix-up by room service."

"No." His voice roughened. "I didn't tell you this guy was wearing a balaclava to hide his face. I doubt he intended even you to see it."

Her head bobbed. "If only I could tell him that I don't remember him."

After a discernible pause, Jack straightened, his arms dropping away from her. "Is that really what you want?"

"To not be wearing a target?" she shot back.

"Don't you think your mother deserves justice?"

Scooting away, Gabby would have sworn she'd find a thin slice oozing blood somewhere on her body. Maybe he hadn't sounded as cutting as she'd thought…but the alternative was contempt. She struggled plenty not to despise herself for sticking to Great-Aunt Isabel's advice. For protecting herself.

"You know…" She stood. "I think I'll skip dinner tonight."

"No." He bent his head and pinched the bridge of his nose between his thumb and forefinger. The regret he showed when he looked up couldn't possibly be fabricated. "I'm such an ass. I stumble over my job sometimes. My…biases. You don't know how frustrating it is when a witness won't talk. Half the time after domestic violence calls, the victim refuses to testify." This all came out raggedly. "We've wasted our time. We *know* he or she'll get hurt again, and we can't do anything."

Still hurt, she said, "*You're* refusing to accept that I don't know anything to tell you. I *want* to remember. I do. But it's not that easy, especially after I've spent a lot of years trying—"

"To forget."

Gabby closed her eyes, feeling the dampness in them. "Yes."

She felt the rush of air when he stood. She still hadn't opened her eyes when he enclosed her in his arms. "I'm sorry. I…don't want to lose the time with you."

She should stick to her guns, but…she didn't want

to lose the limited time she'd have with him, either, so she nodded. "I probably overreacted. Ric has said things like that to me so often over the years. I agreed to this visit partly because I know he's right."

Jack lifted her chin gently with his hand. "He needs family, too, Gabby. You're not the only one scarred by what happened."

She tried to smile, if only to lessen the intensity of the moment. "I know that, too."

He bent his head and kissed her. Not with passion this time, but gently, telling her without words that he understood, that he cared.

She didn't know why, couldn't let herself wonder how much he could care, if only they had time. Right now, she'd take what she could get.

Once he looked down at her again, she found a better smile. "To tell you the truth, I'm really starved."

Jack laughed. "Me, too. Let's go."

Chapter Seven

That evening, Ric took her to dinner in the hotel restaurant—the same place she'd had lunch with Jack today. The very fact that Ric insisted on coming up to her room to get her was a clue that the two men had been talking.

The same host remained on shift and seated them. His eyebrows flickered a little to see her with a different man and she thought there was amusement in his eyes, but she could hardly exclaim loudly, "This one's my brother!"

Once she and Ric had ordered, he commented on her latest near miss. What if she hadn't thought twice about opening the door?

"It was scary," she admitted. In a different way, far more terrifying than having to jump out of the way of a speeding SUV. "Weird, too. I mean, how did he know where I'm staying? What room I'm in?"

"He could have followed you." More slowly, Ric said, "Or me. Probably not Jack."

No, she had a suspicion Jack would have noticed if anyone had tried to follow him.

When she voiced her thought, Ric said, "Yeah, Cowan makes me nervous even at the health club. It's the way he looks at people. He seems to have eyes in the back of his head. You know?"

Gabby wrinkled her nose. "I've noticed. He's hyperaware. It's probably a cop thing."

"I'm sure." He studied her with those dark eyes that reminded her of her father's. "Have you been anywhere on your own that this guy might have picked you up?"

She felt sick enough to hope their meals didn't show up too soon. "I...drove by the house. Actually, I parked across the street from it for a few minutes." Upset, she wouldn't have noticed another car that had stuck with her all the way back to the hotel. "But... he couldn't possibly have been hanging around the house for hours or days waiting for me."

"He sure as hell was determined to get *in* the house," her brother snapped.

They stared at each other for a minute. Gabby wanted to say again how weird all this was, but...it was beginning to seem all too real.

If the killer had seen her at the house and followed her back to the hotel, he wouldn't have known whether she was staying there or just meeting someone for lunch, say. Was it logical that he'd have then broken into the house to find out for sure whether she was staying with her brother or not?

"How did you feel about it?" Ric asked suddenly. Seeing her confusion, he said, "I mean, the house."

Should she opt for honesty? Or pull her punches? No, what was the point in lying?

"I hated looking at it. As far as I could tell, neither you nor Dad has changed a single thing. You haven't painted the house a different color, not even the front door. The arbor is still there, probably with the same roses climbing over it. It was…" She had to look away. "I felt like I was having a flashback."

"That's harsh. The house is white. It's not like it's all that distinctive."

She made herself meet his eyes again, but didn't say a word.

He flushed. "I guess I never think about it. Dad didn't want to change anything, and… I was a kid. Boys don't think about things like remodeling. You know?"

"It's *your* house now. It has been for eight years. What, you still think you're twenty-one and lucky because you don't have to pay rent?"

He groaned and kneaded the back of his neck. "Maybe. Sort of. I did finally remodel the master bedroom and move into it. I put in a Jacuzzi tub. I stayed in my own bedroom longer than I should have. I couldn't bring a woman home with me and explain that, yeah, I slept in a full-size bed because that's all that would fit in the bedroom where I'd grown up."

Gabby was startled into a giggle. "No, that would lead to some awkward questions." She sobered quickly, though. "But…the rest of the house?"

"Dad wanted it to stay the same. The kitchen is really dated, but even though he could have afforded to redo it, he wouldn't hear of it. 'There isn't a damn thing wrong with it,' he'd say."

"Except for the fact that Mom was murdered in that kitchen."

His jaw tightened. "I think he wanted it kept the same as a memorial. Or maybe he deluded himself that she'd walk in the door someday. I don't know."

They were silent, brooding, when their entrées finally appeared. Gabby decided she was hungry enough to eat despite the subject of conversation. In fact, she had several bites before Ric said, "I guess I was trying to honor Dad's wishes."

She nodded. "I can see that. Except…doesn't it bother you?"

"No, my memories are mostly good ones, you know. Dad never let me into the house until it had been cleaned up."

Gabby remembered. She had a vague memory of staying in a hotel, something their family never did. Summer vacations were spent camping. She couldn't remember how long they'd been in the hotel, but she thought at least a week, on top of her hospital stay. Now she guessed the crime scene tape had stayed up for a few days, and afterward…she didn't remember Dad leaving her and Ric, so maybe he'd hired someone to eradicate any remaining evidence of his wife's gory death. Still, wouldn't you think he'd have been reluctant to go home?

She sure was. She'd had hysterics when they'd first returned home. The flash of memory startled her. She'd forgotten her terror.

"Where were you when Mom was killed?" she asked. "Were you in a sports camp or something?"

He flinched, then croaked, "No." He put down his fork. "That's…the worst part for me. I guess I never told you. Dad never knew."

"Told me what?"

Shame infused his voice. "I didn't want you to know."

Unnerved, she waited.

"I was supposed to be home. Do you remember Paul Olsen?"

Supposed to be home. Suddenly short of breath, Gabby couldn't help wondering. If Ric had been there, what would have changed? If the killer had known someone else was in the house, he might not have come in at all, or he might have left without hurting her mother.

Hurting. There was the king of euphemisms.

Or he might have killed Ric, too. Her noisy, nearly hyperactive brother would never have instinctively hidden, the way she did.

Ric reached for her hand. "Gabby?"

"I…" She shook her head. "I'm sorry. What did you say?"

He repeated himself.

"Paul was blond, right?" she asked him.

"Yeah, that was him. Still is, actually. I was at his house, but Mom had told me to be home for lunch. Only, we got this great idea and rode our bikes to the river with a couple of other guys who sneaked away, too."

Her eyes widened. Her eight-year-old brother hadn't been banned from crossing the street, like she was, but he'd had strict limits. The river was at least a mile from home, and to go there without adult supervision...

"You'd have been in so much trouble."

"Yeah." He rolled his shoulders. "We got back to Paul's, and his mother fed us lunch. She thought we'd been down the street at Jeff's. Mom hadn't even called. I thought she'd forgotten." His eyes closed. "She didn't call because she was dead."

And Gabby might still have been huddled in terror in the utility room. She had no idea how long she'd stayed there before she found the courage to slip out the back door and run to old Mrs. Soriano's house, knowing she was practically always home.

Also, Gabby hadn't had to cross the street to get there. Mrs. Soriano lived on the same side and the same block.

"I'm sorry." Ric's Adam's apple bobbed. His hand squeezed Gabby's hard. "I'm sorrier than I can ever say. If I'd been there, like I should have been—"

"You'd probably be dead, too," she said bluntly. "You feel guilty? Get real. You wouldn't have had the sense to hide, and you were old enough to be the kind of witness the police couldn't dismiss."

"You think they dismissed you?"

"I know they did."

"I..." He didn't move for a long moment. He might not even have breathed. "I guess I always thought—"

"It wouldn't have happened if you'd been there."

"Yeah, or I could have hit the guy with my base-ball bat or—" He stopped. "I had a lot of fantasies. I always did *something*. Mom lived, and I could have been a hero, except I'd sneaked away to break all the rules."

"Oh, Ric." Tears prickled in her eyes. "You have no reason to feel guilty. You couldn't have stopped what happened. And think how much worse it would have been if Dad had lost you, too? If I'd had to watch—"

"Yeah." Her big brother cleared his throat. "I never thought about that. I was a kid. I guess… I never got past that."

"I don't think I ever did, either," she admitted, hat-ing the way her voice broke. "A part of me got stuck in that moment."

His eyes were wet, too. "I've been, too, except for me it was a different moment. It was when Mrs. Olsen saw all the police cars and an ambulance with their lights on, and decided they were on our block. She didn't say it was my house—she probably couldn't tell from her front porch. She tried to stop me, but I tore away, jumped on my bike and rode as fast as I could, but when I got there, a police officer grabbed me and told me I couldn't go in. Dad must not have been there yet, or he was and I just didn't see the car, so the officer finally drove me back to the Olsens' house and made me promise to stay there."

"I was at Mrs. Soriano's." From his nod, she saw that he knew that. "By then, I was curled into a shak-ing ball. I remember rocking and rocking and—"

Gabby swallowed. "She tried so hard to reach me, but I think now I was somewhere else."

"You spent a couple of days in the hospital, you know," Ric said slowly. "It took that long before you could talk, tell the cops what you'd seen. Even after…" He frowned. "You didn't really talk much. Before that, you were kind of a motormouth."

"I was, wasn't I?"

"Were you again? I mean, after you went home with Great-Aunt Isabel?"

Gabby shook her head. "I think it was years before I relaxed enough to really talk. Aunt Isabel worried—" She shook her head.

"I've been a butt, haven't I?" His gaze was somber. "I wanted you to make it better, but arresting the killer wouldn't really have made anything better, would it?"

"In a way, it would have. I'll bet you were scared he'd come back, weren't you?"

Rapidly shifting emotions on his face didn't surprise her. Finally his mouth twisted. "Yeah. I never told anyone, but…yeah."

"Also," she said more practically, "I wouldn't have the problem I have now."

"You mean, having someone out to shut you up? Probably not."

That was almost funny…but not quite.

A SINGLE DRIP fell from the man's elbow. Her eyes followed it to the floor. Then came another, and another. *Drip, drip, drip, drip.* Was it raining in here? She turned her face up to the ceiling, then cringed.

Can't move, can't move. He'll see me.

His arm rose and fell. Liquid sprayed upward, a fountain, only the water was a vivid red color. That was why those drips were red. Why the rivulets were scarlet against the black-and-white checkerboard floor. It went on as far as she could see. Now it was threaded with red, as if she could see its veins. *Did floors have veins?* she wondered.

Then she quit wondering anything, because *he* was turning. His eyes met hers, and horror flared to life inside her—

GASPING, GABBY BOLTED AWAKE. Oh, God—that had been the most vivid nightmare she'd had in ages. The colors… Yet it was fading already, even as she tried to hold on to it.

The floor, veined like the human body. He saw her. The vivid shade of red.

He hadn't really seen her. Gabby felt sure of that, or he'd have killed her, too. Dreams were most often nonsensical, combining bits and pieces of recent events or thoughts or fears, but a nightmare could also warp memories.

Dripping. What had been dripping in the dream? She was almost grateful the nightmare was slipping away. All these years, and they kept returning. Not always the same, but she knew, she *knew*, they were about Mom's murder.

Shuddering, she rolled onto her back. Her nightgown felt like a boa constrictor squeezing her. Her teeth actually chattered when she sat up to untangle the fabric. It felt chilly here in the room, probably because she was sweating and her nightgown was damp. Maybe she should just get dressed. She couldn't imagine falling asleep again.

Gabby looked at the glowing numbers on the clock. 4:37. She'd be exhausted later in the day if she didn't get some more sleep…except it wasn't like anything would stop her from going to bed early tonight.

Her eye fell on the black slab of her phone lying on the end table. She'd spent a lifetime suffering the nightmares and their aftereffects in silence. Even at five and six years old, after she'd gone to live with Aunt Isabel, Gabby had never cried out aloud, never slipped from her bed to sneak into her aunt's for comfort. She remembered telling Ric that it took years for her to be able to chatter at all normally. From the minute she'd told herself she had to be quiet in the utility room, she couldn't make a sound, she hadn't been able to relax and think, *It's okay now*. It wasn't okay.

Since coming back to Leclaire to get to know her brother and face her fears, she'd discovered nothing was okay. The killer was still here, not two steps away. His hands wouldn't still be bloody—they'd look like anyone else's—but she saw the dripping, as if out of the corner of her eye.

Blood. That's what had been dripping.

Her arms wrapped herself as tightly as she could manage while she resisted the pull to pick up the phone. For the first time in her life, she wanted to hear someone else's voice.

Jack's.

She wanted his arms around her, too. She wanted him murmuring reassurances even as rage underlaid every word. *He'd* keep her safe.

But she didn't reach for the phone. Couldn't. He'd talk to her, she knew; come to her, if that's what she wanted. But letting herself rely on someone else would only weaken her. In a few days or weeks, she'd leave town, and be alone again.

Once she was far away, these maddening nightmares would recede again, become only occasional. This one had been so shockingly real only because, thanks to Ric and even Jack, she'd been remembering.

She should be celebrating. This was the biggest reason for her visit. Those memories were coming back to her, just as she wanted.

And they were every bit as horrifying as she'd feared.

BY SATURDAY, Jack had cleared enough of his other cases to focus solely on the Ortiz murder. Given the window of opportunity, he checked out every scrap of information available from Evidence, excepting the victim's slashed, blood-soaked garments. Those, he didn't need to see. If he found a viable suspect, that might change; DNA recovery and tracing had come a long way, and he couldn't imagine that the killer hadn't cut himself, too, given his frenzy. Chances were excellent that tiny spots of blood that weren't Colleen Ortiz's would be found. At the moment, that wouldn't be helpful. Sure, the DNA could be entered into online databases to search for a forensic hit or even offender match—but Jack didn't believe for a second that this killer would be found there. He hadn't been a wandering serial killer. Colleen had known him.

The murder weapon wasn't here, either, presumably because the killer had brought it with him and taken it away when he was done. No knife with the right kind of blade had been missing from the Ortiz kitchen.

Most of this, he'd already accessed on his computer, but it was past time to look for holes in the original investigation. He was determined to dig deeper, starting with anything that *hadn't* been included in reports. Tapes of interviews had been transcribed, but he'd listen to them anyway. There could be a scrap of paper with a forgotten bit of information from a phone conversation. He wanted to see who, besides his father, had been even briefly considered to be a suspect. Why hadn't there been other witnesses? Hadn't a single neighbor within earshot of what had to be terrible screams been home?

He plunged in, impervious to the comings and goings and voices of surrounding coworkers.

After the murder, of course, neighbors at least a block in every direction had been canvassed.

Nobody had seen the killer come or go. Except for a couple of seniors, people in the nearest houses had been at work, kids in summer camps or daycare. The old lady Gabby had run to didn't have good vision, and had been five houses away. The old guy next door—the same one who snatched Gabby from the path of the speeding car—had been napping. He'd heard what must have been the screams and was only annoyed, figuring they came from the teenagers at a house behind him who had been playing loud music, partying, yelling and generally making a nuisance of themselves that summer while their parents were at work.

The greatest mystery was how the killer had left the house without leaving a trail of blood and bloody footprints. He hadn't gone out through the garage, thank God, because if he had he'd have passed through the utility room and been inches from the little girl hiding under a sheet. Instead, he must have used the back door.

Speculation at the time—and Jack wouldn't argue—was that the killer had parked at the side of the house. Raul Ortiz owned a small utility trailer kept in the backyard, hidden behind gates in the fence. But a dirt lane from the street led to those gates. The killer's vehicle would have been a lot less visible there, unless the old man next door had looked out the window in his garage—which he hadn't.

But why hadn't the guy left bloody footprints on his way out? Some remnants of blood were found in the kitchen sink, but not in large quantities. There was no hint he'd gone upstairs or taken a shower.

Jack brooded over the problem for a few minutes. Something like coveralls was the obvious answer. A Tyvek suit, hood off when he entered, pulled over his head to protect himself from blood spatter as he stabbed the victim. Or even the kind of coveralls workers sometimes wore, paired with rubber boots, say. Strip it all off, bundle it into a plastic bag, and walk out.

But Gabby had said the man wore blue. Had both the coveralls and the clothes he wore beneath been blue?

Frowning, Jack continued.

A woman named Margaret Vaughn had lived across the street from the Ortiz home. She'd been shopping the afternoon of the murder, but she'd reported seeing a man in a blue uniform ringing the doorbell the day before the murder. He'd caught her eye mainly because he wasn't carrying a clipboard, a package or any equipment, and he'd knocked after there was no response to the doorbell. Even then, she didn't think anything about it; his van was parked in the driveway, and she'd been sure it had a business name emblazoned on the side. Cowan something, she thought.

If Margaret Vaughn hadn't witnessed Jack's father on the Ortiz doorstep, his life wouldn't have been ruined.

How could Jack blame her, though? That was exactly the kind of tidbit that led to arrests.

He perused notes from multiple interviews, mostly with other men who'd been at the house previously. The investigators had favored friends of Raul and Colleen. They'd spoken to an insurance agent who'd come out to give them a quote. One of the detectives commented that Raul seemed to handle most repairs around the house. The furnace seemed to be an exception.

Finally, Jack plugged in the tape player he'd borrowed from the tech gurus and began listening to interviews. He jotted notes on what his father said in several interviews then. It had stayed consistent. How much of it would Dad remember now?

Only then, with deep reluctance, did he pop in the tape labeled Gabriella Ortiz #1.

Chapter Eight

Hearing the small, high, faltering voice made him feel as if he'd swallowed battery acid.

Jack couldn't help noticing that Gabby sounded even younger than she'd actually been, which shouldn't have come as a surprise. Reverting after trauma was a typical response in a child, one that investigators should have kept in mind.

The first interviewer, a detective named Scott Hudson who was long since retired, had tried to sound sympathetic, but Jack suspected he didn't have any children of his own, because he wasn't good at it.

"Mommy looked so scared," four-year-old Gabby whispered. "I didn't know why."

"Was the man already there when she looked scared?"

Silence. Jack's gaze dropped to the transcript, where someone had noted: (Nodded)

"Did your mommy let the man in through the front door?"

(Confusion)

"Did you *see* the man come into the house?" A

hint of irritation was creeping into Detective Hudson's voice.

"Uh-uh. I heard Mommy yelling. Like when she's mad at Ric."

"Your brother."

"Uh-huh."

"Did you hear what she said?"

"I… I don't know." Gabby was whispering again.

"Can you try to remember?" Hudson asked more aggressively.

"She said 'What're you doing here?'"

"That's it?"

(Hunched. Teeth chattering)

Jack paused the tape, rolled his head, then his shoulders. He'd *seen* her hunch over like that. That time at the restaurant. Her teeth weren't chattering, but…damn. That wasn't hard to picture.

Hudson pressed her harder about what she'd heard and got nothing. Finally, he shifted to, "What did the man look like?"

The chattering teeth could be heard on the tape, unless Jack was imagining things, followed by a tiny whisper. "I don't know."

He finally extracted from her the information Jack already knew, that the man had blue pants and shirt.

By that time Gabby was crying. Hudson had to give up.

Bothered by something he couldn't put a finger on, Jack rewound the tape. In attempting to get a description, the detective said, "The man must have walked right by the doorway into the utility room. Close to you."

(Shaking)

"You could see what he was wearing."

(Nod)

"Can you tell me?"

Silence. No transcript notes.

In one of her more coherent answers, Gabby said, "That man had blue pants and a blue shirt. And black shoes."

Whoa. Jack rewound again, intently listening for the slight emphasis apparently no one else had noticed.

"*That* man had blue pants and a blue shirt."

Had she seen *two* men? Why the hell hadn't anyone asked? A single killer still seemed likeliest—multiple stabbings almost always meant anger and a personal motivation. If that was the case, had Gabby seen the man in something like a Tyvek suit and not realized he was the same man who walked out past her, almost close enough to touch?

Would it help to know what he'd worn during the murder? Maybe, maybe not. But, damn, Hudson's interview had been incompetent, to put it kindly.

In the ensuing days, two other investigators went at it, neither with any more skill. By the second interview, Gabby didn't remember anything her mom said. She remembered blood. That memory ended interview number two.

By number three, five days after the murder, Gabby said, "He kept hitting Mommy, and hitting her and hitting her! An' yelling at her!" Her voice rose with each repetition until it was almost a scream. "And I wanted to hit him, 'cept…"

She was a little girl, and terrified.

"What was he yelling?"

"She ruined something. But Mommy wouldn't."

Why hadn't those idiots found a woman to interview their young witness? Or at least a kindly father of little girls? Why hadn't they gently asked simple, specific questions, like, "What color hair did the man have? Was it brown like mine? Black like yours?"

No—to be fair, detective number two had asked that. He just waited until she was already sobbing after their discussion of the blood.

Why hadn't they sat her down with her father, and let *him* ask the questions?

All three investigators had concluded, and so noted, that "witness is too young to provide reliable information."

Had Raul Ortiz ever talked to Gabby about what she'd seen? If so, had she been so confused by then, he hadn't gotten anything useful? Or had he tried to tell one of the investigators what she saw and was blown off?

Frustrated and angry, Jack wouldn't be surprised if that was exactly what happened. But, damn it, wouldn't Raul have told someone else? Ric would have been too young then, but later?

The detectives had sought out the victim's friends, but all of them insisted she hadn't said anything about a man who made her uneasy.

The killer hadn't raped her. Hadn't stolen anything from the house that day so far as investigators could tell, unless it was inconsequential, a memento. Hadn't thought to look for Colleen's young daughter—or didn't know she had one until later.

Colleen hadn't just screamed, "Get out!" Hard not to conclude that she'd known her killer. But how? And was he someone she'd met recently?

Or someone she'd known from her past?

"JACK." HIS FATHER sounded pleased to hear from him that evening. "It's been a while. Something new?"

"Yeah." He cleared his throat and kicked back in his recliner, gazing at the blank television. Bluntness came naturally to him. "I've gotten permission to open a cold case. Colleen Ortiz's murder."

The silence was deafening. When his father finally spoke, it was hoarsely. "You can't rewrite history."

"I can if I put a name to the killer. If I arrest him."

"If you're doing this for me, don't."

"I'm not." Jack sat up straight and put his feet on the floor. Where in hell had that come from? Of course his lifelong quest had to do with clearing his father's name once and for all.

But things had changed, he realized, when he got to know Gabby. Ric, too, to some extent. *They* needed closure, and deserved it.

A grunt told him Dad didn't believe him.

"How do you expect to learn anything the original investigators couldn't?" his father asked. "Neighbors have moved, died, forgotten whatever they once knew. I heard Raul Ortiz died a few years back. Who is left? The kids?"

"The youngest is thirty now. The son still lives in the house." He paused. "I reopened the case because the Ortiz girl just came back to Leclaire for a visit."

"They talked to her then. For God's sake, Jack, she was a little girl! What do you think she can tell you?"

"She's already told me some things," he said in a harder voice than he'd intended. "Among them, she admits she's spent her entire life haunted by what happened, and by what she witnessed. Turns out her brother, Ric, feels the same, even though he escaped seeing his mother killed or even the house before it was cleaned. For him, he went off to hang out with friends, and his whole world changed. Next thing he knew, his little sister was yanked away. Did you know he hasn't seen her in over twenty years?"

"You're angry."

"Yeah, I am. I always have been. I lost *my* family because you were unfairly looked at for that murder."

"No. Things are never that simple. You know that."

He did. If his parents' relationship had been tight, Mom would have supported Dad and nothing would have changed for him. As it was, there might well have been a divorce in the next few years, anyway, but that wouldn't have been the same. His parents would have traded kids for visits, Mom might have stayed in the area, and Kristine and he wouldn't have had to choose between Mom and Dad.

"The murder was a dividing line."

"It was that," his father admitted sadly.

Part of Jack wanted to push until Dad admitted what had been wrong, why the split had been so bitter. But he took a deep breath, closed his eyes and reminded himself he could do that anytime. Maybe over Christmas, which he usually spent with his father. Right now, his driving goal was to identify Colleen Ortiz's murderer. And one of the first steps was to interview again anyone who'd had knowledge pertaining to the crime.

That included Brian Cowan, the only serious suspect in her murder.

"I've been listening to the tapes of the interviews," Jack said. "I wanted to hear the subtleties that don't show up in a transcript. The investigators took most of the obvious steps, but the interviews with Gabby Ortiz were a joke. I have the impression they dismissed her as too young to be any use even before they talked to her. She was a traumatized child, and they didn't even try to ask questions in a way she'd understand. Instead, they pushed her into crying and gave up. I think Gabby saw plenty, and I think she can still pull those memories out of hiding."

He winced at how grimly determined he sounded. Was he any better than the jackasses who'd further traumatized her? What was he going to do, crack open her head and yank the memories out even if he left irreparable damage behind?

Jack squeezed the back of his neck. His muscles had knots on top of knots.

Damn it, that's not how it would be. He had to believe she'd be *glad* to get it all out in the open.

But he knew he might be kidding himself. Cops had to be ruthless. They couldn't tiptoe around the sensibilities of witnesses and suspects, or they'd never arrive at the truth. A few faces in particular flashed past his eyes. Right this minute, he didn't much like himself.

"I met her," his father said. "Gabriella."

Jack's hand dropped from his neck. "I didn't know that."

"I worked on the furnace pretty close to a week before the murder. She was a curious little girl. Her mother kept telling her to leave me alone to do my job, but I told her I didn't mind. She was smart. Her questions were sharp for a kid that age." There might be a smile in his father's voice. "Cute, too, with those pigtails and bright eyes. Hell, you must have known her."

"I remember seeing her around, but that's all."

He saw her now. Disconcertingly so.

"What I really called for is to ask you to tell me again what you overheard that bothered you enough to feel like you should go back to check on a woman you didn't really know."

His father surprised him once again. "I'd done maintenance on their furnace several times over the years. It was getting old, but they didn't feel like they could afford a new one. Anyway, I'd talked to Colleen and her husband both before."

Why didn't the notes from his father's interview mention that? Was it possible he'd made a move on Colleen? No, if he had, she or her husband would probably have called another furnace company. Unless Dad and Colleen had actually had consensual sex… But, again, Jack found himself shaking his head. There was nothing in Dad's tone to suggest anything like that. Gabby would have been around on previous visits, too.

"Nice lady," his father added, "which is partly why I worried. I should have stopped by or called sooner. I talked it over with your mother, but she thought I was making a mountain out of a molehill."

Until it turned out that Jack's mother was very wrong.

"I was just coming up the steps from the basement when I heard her say something like, 'You saw me.' She sounded…alarmed."

Had Colleen been doing something she shouldn't have? Or could she have seen the killer, someone who scared her, and hoped he hadn't seen her?

"I got to the top of the steps and could see that she was on the phone. She had her back to me, or she'd have probably moved out of earshot. Instead, she snapped, 'If you keep bothering me, you should know I kept evidence. I won't hesitate to take it to the police.' Her voice was shrill. That's when she turned and realized she wasn't alone. She said goodbye and hung up the phone. Even while she was writing a check for me and chatting, I could tell she was upset. I asked if she was okay, and she said of course. What could I do? But…it just stuck in my mind. You know? She had evidence of a crime? That's what it sounded like."

Dad was right. That *was* what it sounded like. And Jack thought her threat had been a bad idea.

And then he had another thought. What if the intruder in Ric's house hadn't been checking to find out whether Gabby was staying there? What if, now that she was in town, he'd gotten worried about that evidence? Assuming he hadn't found it twenty-five years ago—and there'd been no sign the house had been tossed—he might have figured nobody would recognize that evidence. But now Gabby was home. She might know something—or her brother might hand over some of their mother's things because he thought she'd want them. So he'd gone through the house and found nothing except Christmas ornaments stored there. He didn't know about the storage facility. And, damn, Jack had to be very sure nobody followed Ric and Gabby there when they got around to looking through the stuff. He also fully intended to go with them and stand guard.

He'd have to finesse any explanation of why he needed to accompany them, but he'd manage.

AT THE HEAD of the driveway, Gabby's feet refused to move. Easier to decide she was going to walk through the house with her brother than to actually do it.

"You just going to stand there forever?" Ric asked from the porch steps.

She glared at him.

His eyebrows arched. "You're the one who wanted to get it over with."

"Why do I have to do it at all?" Gosh, maybe because revisiting her childhood home in hopes it would spark memories was part of what she'd been determined to accomplish?

"You don't," her brother said reasonably. "But wouldn't seeing the indoors looking normal and lived-in help wipe out your bad memories?"

He was right, except—"Yeah, good plan, if you and Dad hadn't kept the house as a damn shrine."

Although, the fact that they had might be a good thing, it occurred to her. The house served as a visual aide in her memory recovery process.

Ric kept scanning the block. "Let's not stand out here. It's cold."

His eyes darted back and forth as if he expected—what? A gunshot? *She* hadn't even known what that ping of metal off metal had meant when she'd been a child, or why Dad had grabbed her and Ric and all but thrown them behind the car and covered them with his body. Tires had squealed, but he hadn't moved until a police car pulled up. Witnesses hadn't heard a shot, either, which meant the gunman had used a silencer—actually, as Gabby had since learned, a suppressor. Gang members sometimes did, the officer had said, looking suspiciously at her father. Even she hadn't liked the way that policeman had studied Daddy.

"You're right," she agreed now. She'd take the grand tour. Wasn't seeing her home part of why she'd come back to Leclaire at last?

By the time she reached the porch, Ric had unlocked and opened the front door. Despite her resolve, she felt as if she were wading waist deep in a river, the current pushing back as she tried to walk forward. The spirit was willing, but the flesh was weak. Or was it the other way around?

To her relief, seeing the living room was okay. The hardwood floor must have been refinished at some point because she remembered it more scuffed and scratched. She and Ric had been hard on it.

Fireplace—check. The big flat screen TV was a major step up from the crappy color TV they'd had then. The new one was accompanied by the usual cable box and high-tech equipment, including a tangle of wires. Ric had to be the one who'd added a serious stereo system and speakers, too.

She didn't remember the sofa, either, but had an uneasy feeling the recliner might be the same one, albeit reupholstered. Her gaze slid right past the coffee table, too.

"You actually have fires in here," she said, nodding at the fireplace. When she was a little girl, they used it only when the power was out. But a pile of newspapers, a wrought-iron wood holder and fireplace tools on the hearth made her think that was no longer the case. There was even a handsome screen and a colorful hearth rug.

"Yeah, Mom didn't like smoke, and Dad—I don't know, he just never built one, but I like having a fire at this time of year."

She smiled at him. "I would, too, if I wasn't always living in an apartment."

"I could make dinner for you some night. We could roast s'mores."

Gabby laughed, feeling way more relaxed. "Maybe."

Maybe not, she thought when her brother led the way past the dining room and into the kitchen. Forget "maybe not." "Not even on a cold day in hell" was more accurate.

Setting eyes on that damn checkerboard vinyl, she actually recoiled. "Oh, God."

Ric turned. "Oh, God what?"

It was like stepping into her most recent nightmare, the details of which she'd have sworn she'd forgotten. The endless black-and-white checkerboard floor with rivulets of blood everywhere. No, veins, as if skin had been peeled back from human flesh.

She shuffled backward even as she stared incredulously at a kitchen essentially unchanged from that hideous day. Wood cabinets painted white, white porcelain sink, bar stools with natural wood seats and white-painted legs. White eyelet curtains.

Out of the corner of her eye, she saw the doorway into the utility room. That's where she'd hidden, crouched behind the laundry basket with a sheet pulled over herself except for the fold that allowed her to see.

Drip, drip, drip.

Chapter Nine

She couldn't seem to wrench her gaze away from where her mother had died. "This is far enough." She didn't need to open cupboard doors to find out if the cereal was on the same shelf.

"It's been twenty-five years!" her brother exclaimed. "We've replaced the floor. Dad had to buy new bar stools—"

Because at least one had been splintered into pieces, and the others almost had to have been splattered with their mother's blood.

Nausea rose to choke her. She whirled and ran for the small downstairs bathroom, bringing up her breakfast in the toilet. Then she stood shakily in front of the sink and rinsed her mouth with handfuls of water. The strength of her reaction appalled her.

Ric's long arm reached past her. He took a bottle of mouthwash from the medicine cabinet and handed it to her.

She rinsed, then stared at herself in the mirror. She was too pale, and her eyes looked curiously blank. A thousand-yard stare. She'd read that description before, and knew it fit.

Ric's hand on her shoulder pulled her back to herself. "Why don't we go upstairs?" he suggested, tone subdued. "Master bedroom and bathroom have been been redone."

She nodded.

The staircase was familiar, of course, but had no bad associations. The first bedroom had been Ric's, and was now painted white instead of…green was what she remembered. It held a double bed, not the twin one he'd had the last time she saw it. Yeah, this room wouldn't impress any women he brought home, she thought with a welcome flicker of humor.

Her bedroom was still pink, but otherwise so bare, there wasn't anything to react to, not even a bed.

"I think your dresser might be in storage," he said awkwardly.

Gabby nodded.

Linen closet—he didn't open the door. When they played hide-and-seek, she'd sometimes used the closet, but he always found her right away.

Bathroom—not really changed, but it had always been plain. No wallpaper, not even a border. *She'd* wanted Mommy to paint it pink, too, but Ric got mad, so it stayed cream-colored with standard white fixtures.

Ric had obviously claimed Mom and Dad's bedroom, because she didn't recognize a thing except the placement of the closets, window and door to the second bathroom.

"King-size bed," she murmured.

His grin looked forced. "Of course."

"You have a TV in your bedroom. Remember when you said you wanted one? One of your friends got to have one, and a game console, too."

"Nintendo. Man, I wanted that," he said reminiscently. "Mom said I couldn't go to Tony's house anymore."

Hearing his smugness and guessing how much time he'd undoubtedly spent there, she laughed. Ric, at least, had been allowed to run wild within the neighborhood. She'd never had that chance. Maybe she never would have, even if she'd stayed with Dad and Ric. After Mom was murdered, their father would have locked them down.

Gabby would be grateful to Aunt Isabel for the rest of her life. How could she have stayed in this house?

She pulled her wandering thoughts back. How strange it was that she could see Mom glowering at Ric, her hands planted on her hips and her eyes narrowed, and feel no more than the warmth of a memory.

Gabby went to the window and lifted the blinds to look out at the backyard. Dad used to have a vegetable garden at one end, and he'd improvised a batting cage for Ric to practice hitting. She remembered the crab apple tree, beautiful in bloom but hard on Dad's attempts to keep a lawn growing beneath it.

"The fence needs replacing," she commented.

"Yeah, yeah."

"I guess you don't garden, huh?"

He grimaced. "I try to keep up the front yard. And I mow."

The flower bed in front was currently bare, frozen earth, of course, except for the sticks of what were probably a few roses. And the climbers tied to the arbor close to the sidewalk. That almost had to have been rebuilt, it occurred to her, although of course it was unchanged from her memories.

"I'm done," she declared. "I've seen all I want to see."

"I'm sorry." His regretful dark eyes met hers. "I guess thinking you'd stay here wasn't realistic, was it?"

"Maybe if the whole house had been drastically remodeled, but I'm not even sure about that," she admitted.

"Listen, I was hoping you'd take a few hours to go through the stuff in storage with me. I've been paying for the unit ever since Dad died, and I don't even know what's in it. We can probably get rid of most of it, and I can move the rest to the garage."

"Sure, I can do that. Do you want to go this afternoon?"

"Why don't I take tomorrow off instead? I think this qualifies as a personal day."

Once they were downstairs, she averted her eyes so she didn't have to see the kitchen again. Ric insisted on stepping outside first and taking a careful look around before letting her join him. Had Jack given him basic bodyguard instructions?

Once they were in his SUV and he'd fired it up,

he said, "If I decide to stay in the house, I'm having the kitchen ripped down to the studs and remodeled." He added on a burst of anger, "To hell with Dad."

She laid a hand over Ric's, white-knuckled on the steering wheel. Neither said another word about the house.

JACK HAD HOPED to spend Monday with Gabby, but this wasn't quite what he'd had in mind. For one thing, he'd envisioned the two of them together, not the three of them.

Building trust was the idea. Today's outing to the storage facility instead had him in his Tahoe, trailing a block behind Ric's vehicle, keeping adequate distance to be sure no one else was following them. Once they got there and slid open the metal door into the unit, which faced the street, his role was to stand guard, obviously armed.

Damn, he wished this had been an internal unit in one of the more modern facilities, but according to Ric, his dad had rented this one not that long after his wife's death. Storage facilities were a lot more stripped down in those days. Someone passing on the street would be able to catch a glimpse into the unit, which he didn't like.

He was dismayed to see how much was crammed in here, although it became apparent that furniture provided the bulk.

Neither Ric nor Gabby wanted to keep any of the furniture.

A black pickup truck with a canopy slowed on the

street and turned into the facility. The gate slid open, which meant the driver had a code. Jack watched as it headed for a different aisle. After waiting a minute, he strolled far enough to see that it had stopped in front of a unit, and a man and woman were already unloading some apparently heavy plastic tubs to add to whatever they'd already stashed.

He shook his head and went back to his position in front of the Ortiz unit. Ric and Gabby had come up with a system by now; everything to get rid of that was too big to go in the back of Ric's SUV was being moved to one side of the unit, potential keepers to the other side.

Since they had to work their way toward the back wall, the stuff spilled out onto the concrete in front of the unit and leaned against fenders. More of a screen, letting him relax a little.

When Ric passed him carrying a scratched end table, Jack said, "You can load the back of my Tahoe, too, if you want. Why don't you put the stuff for the dump in my vehicle? I don't mind taking it."

"Thanks. That would help. I can run by the thrift store."

Gabby approaching carrying a ratty artificial Christmas tree in a torn black plastic bag. After putting it in the bed of his truck, she grinned at him. "I'm sure I speak for Ric, too, when I say that if you see anything you really like, feel free to keep it." She bumped his hip with hers and went back the way she'd come, leaving him smiling.

Things slowed down when she and her brother started opening boxes and going through the contents.

Jack felt edgy, needing to keep an eye both on the street and anyone entering the facility, but also on what Ric and Gabby were handling. Would they recognize the "evidence" Colleen had used to threaten her killer? Or had she made it up, and there never was any such thing? If it was real…what could it be?

If she'd taken a photo showing something incriminating—say, two men together who shouldn't have been—her son and daughter would undoubtedly toss it. He assumed they'd keep family photos, but ones of strangers? That was the kind of crap people left for their children to throw out.

He wanted to look at all the photos. He might recognize someone Ric wouldn't. It would be really helpful if Gabby gasped and cried, "That's him! Oh, my God, that's him!"

Jack wished he knew whether she'd seen the killer's face or not.

They worked until almost two o'clock, anxious to finish. The "keep" pile was pathetically small after two-thirds of the things their father had thought should be saved for posterity had been packed in one or the other SUV, destined respectively for the dump or the thrift store.

Jack, of course, had every intention of taking the discarded stuff home with him. He'd at least look through the boxes of smaller stuff, paper and photos. What little the brother and sister wanted to keep was to remain in storage temporarily. Ric planned to come back for it and close out the locker. It should be safe enough. Jack could ask to go through it later.

When? a voice murmured in his head. *After Gabby's gone?*

He didn't want her going anywhere.

He rode Ric's bumper on the way to a nearby café, where they took a booth and ordered.

Jack's fingers and face started tingling as the warmth penetrated. Gabby gave an exaggerated shiver. "That was fun."

"You could have come in the summer," Ric pointed out.

Her expression closed. "This was…a good time for me to take a break."

Did Ric still not know she'd quit her last job and was completely at loose ends right now? Jack started speculating on whether there might be a suitable opening at a local college. Even if a major university wouldn't hire her without the PhD, there were plenty of community colleges, both here in the Spokane area and across the border in Idaho. What if he suggested she looked?

"You know, that was actually kind of depressing," she said suddenly. "I mean, did Dad really think he was saving treasures for us?"

Ric sighed and rubbed a hand over his jaw. "No, I think with Mom gone, he just wanted a lot of stuff out of sight. Probably out of mind."

Sounding doubtful, Gabby said, "There wasn't much there that was hers that seemed personal. You know?"

"No. Well, family pictures."

"That's true." She wrinkled her nose. "Well, if he was going for the 'out of mind' goal, he wouldn't have encased the house in amber."

Her brother looked disturbed. "Maybe Dad just hated a messy garage."

"There is the basement."

Ric shook his head. "Remember that time it flooded? What little was down there got ruined."

Jack hadn't noticed a door leading to a basement, and was annoyed with himself. "Isn't the furnace down there?" he asked, as if he didn't know.

"Yeah, but it was installed on a concrete pedestal, so it was okay. The basement is only a partial, anyway. It sits under maybe half the house."

"Well, you'll have room for what you're saving in the garage, but everything that was in storage would have taken up most of it."

"Yeah, Dad never did like clutter."

Jack saw a fleeting expression on Gabby's face that cramped his chest. Sadness. Grief. Not having to do with the stuff they'd gone through today, he guessed, but with the fact that there had to be a lot about her father she'd forgotten, or never known.

Ric showed no signs of noticing. Jack increasingly thought of him as a friend—but in holding on to his anger, Ric had been more than a little insensitive to his sister's feelings.

Jack grimaced. Like he was anyone to judge, given that he'd been using and manipulating both of them.

Guilt pierced him again, but he was doing this for the right reasons.

He just wished he thought Gabby would see it that way.

"WHEN DID YOUR parents get divorced?" Gabby asked, being nosy but figuring her question wasn't unreasonable considering how much Jack knew about her life. She licked her fingers. Barbeque was messy.

Ric had claimed to have a date tonight. She didn't know whether to believe him or not. Maybe he'd just had enough of her company today. Truthfully, the tour of the house yesterday and the hours today spent sifting through the detritus of their past had been pretty intense. She was kind of glad to have a break from her brother, so she didn't blame him if he felt the same.

Of course, that left Jack stuck with asking her out, but she'd have said no if she'd gotten any vibe that he didn't actually want to spend the evening with her. He did say he'd have made dinner for them at home, except he hadn't grocery shopped all week. Red had tinged the angular line of his cheekbones when he said that, which made her wonder.

It was just as well, though. Being alone with him in his place would have challenged her ability to resist temptation. She'd have ended up in bed with him, and her deepest instincts said that this was too soon even if she wanted to disregard her fear of feeling too much for him, given that a future together was really unlikely.

Jack's eyes darkened as he watched her trying not

to drip sauce down her front. More than that, a glint in those eyes told her he was aroused. Um, maybe that had to do with her licking her fingers. She grabbed a wad of napkins.

He pulled his gaze away, looked down at his own plateful of ribs, and reached for one. "Ah, I don't know if I said this, but my parents split not that long after your mom died."

"Really? Did you expect it?"

He shook his head. "I was a kid. They weren't yelling at each other, so what'd I know?" He tore meat off the bone with strong white teeth and demolished the rib in no time. His cleanup was more efficient than hers. "You know my father was briefly looked at for your mother's murder," he said abruptly.

She stared at him. "No. Once I was twenty or so, I pulled up all the articles I could find on the investigation, but there was never anything about that. I thought they'd never identified any suspects."

"I'm surprised. It was common knowledge around here. You know how people talk."

Gabby nodded. Wow, was this weird, or what? "Dad wouldn't have told me anything like that when he called. If he was more open with Aunt Isabel, she wouldn't have passed on anything he said."

"That makes sense."

"It was mostly your mother who drove the carpool, wasn't it?"

"Yeah, the only job she had was doing the bookkeeping for Dad's business. You might remember him. He had a furnace repair business. He came out to your house something like a week before your mother was killed."

She frowned. "I don't know why I remember that, but I do. He was nice. Most people got tired of my questions really fast, but he didn't." She studied him. "You look a lot like him, don't you?"

He shifted in a way that suggested discomfort. "People say so. I never think about it." He eyed her. "You don't exactly look like either of your parents."

"Maybe not my face, but obviously I got the black hair from Dad, but my eyes and lighter skin from Mom. I can see Dad when I look at Ric except he got Mom's height and, wouldn't you know, I got the short genes from Dad's side of the family." She still felt aggrieved about that. "His mother wasn't even five feet tall."

Jack obviously wanted to smile, but didn't. "How tall are you?"

She scrunched up her nose. "I claim five foot three, but my doctor says five foot two and a half."

Something about the way she said that made him laugh.

When her heart skipped a few beats, she decided to get back to the original topic of conversation.

"So, why did the police even consider your father back then? Just because he'd been at the house so recently?"

"Partly." He seemed to be watching her closely. "You described the killer as wearing all blue, too. His uniform was navy blue."

"I remember saying that."

"You don't sound so sure."

Gabby refused to give away her discomfort with body language. All she said was, "It's hazy." Except something tickled at her. She just didn't know what.

His hand closed over hers. His warmth and strength anchored her. She just hoped her hand wasn't greasy.

"Hey. I'm sorry. I wasn't trying to go there."

Wasn't he? Yet somehow he kept circling back to her mother's murder. Maybe it was the cop in him, or maybe that was just natural, given that it reared so hugely in both their memories. And then a thought struck her.

"How could the police talking to your father have anything to do with your parents breaking up?"

"I don't know how much it did. I think my mom was embarrassed by the gossip. From things he's said, there were already fractures. He's never been willing to talk about it, and neither was she." His expression closed down. "I don't have much of a relationship with my mother."

"I'm sorry." Gabby squeezed his hand, hoping she returned some of the comfort he'd offered her. "It would almost be easier to have parents break up if they'd been fighting or…or if there was abuse. Then it might be a relief instead of a shock."

He grimaced. "Maybe."

They both ate in silence for a minute. When he spoke again, it was to ask more about her aunt taking her away, and whether Gabby had had any understanding of what was happening.

As she answered, Gabby thought about how different this was from her typical dates. It felt as if they were truly opening up with each other. Sharing the experiences that made them the people they were, instead of sticking with superficialities. Of course, they'd never been strangers to each other, even though she didn't remember him ever saying a word to her when they were children. Why would he? She was just a way younger sibling. Ric probably grumbled about her to his friends. Still, they had in common a time and place...and it sounded as if her mom's murder might have had an impact on his parents' divorce. Which bothered her on some level she didn't want to think about.

It was easy to segue from talking about her stern but loving aunt to that never-ending dissertation.

Of course, at the end of the evening Jack walked her up to her room, and insisted on "clearing it" before she could do more than hover in the doorway.

"Bathroom is secure," he reported with a lopsided grin as stepped past her and allowed her to back into the room.

Her "good to know" sounded a little breathless. His eyes were intense, heated, and she knew he'd retreated into the hall to give her more choice about what happened next.

"Gabby?"

His low, husky voice played a chord low in her belly. She quivered, stepped forward and flung her arms around his neck.

Jack growled something, she had no idea what, and kissed her. One of his hands wrapped her neck, the other covered her hip and buttock so he could lift her. His tongue was in her mouth, the ridge of his erection pressed against her stomach. Gabby wanted to climb him, wrap her legs around his waist. She wanted…

He swung her in a slow circle. Her shoulder collided with the door frame, but she didn't care. She ended up plastered against the short section of wall that formed an entry to her hotel room, Jack's long, hard body pinning her. His hands roved, and she held on for dear life.

Every so often, he lifted his head to let them both breathe, the blaze of his eyes making her shudder. But this time, his gaze flicked to the side, and Gabby knew: he was looking at the bed. And, even as longing cramped low in her belly, all her qualms ignited, too.

She pushed against him, and he fell back, something like shock on his face. Had he been that sure of her?

"Good night." Not feeling coherent, the one word was the best she could manage, and there might have been a tremor in her voice.

Jack gave his head a small shake and said hoarsely, "Yeah. I'll, uh, check in tomorrow."

After closing the door, leaving him out in the hall, she couldn't remember if she'd said another word.

Chapter Ten

Jack drove home in distinct discomfort. He'd let that kiss get out of hand, partly because they'd been standing in the open doorway of Gabby's hotel room. A corner of the bed was in sight. And, damn, he knew she wanted him, too. She had tried hard to meld her body to his while he kissed her until he couldn't think about anything but her taste and her generous breasts pressed to his chest and the feel of her nicely rounded hip enclosed in his hand.

Braking now at a red light, he bumped his head against the steering wheel a couple of times. Thank God she'd come to her senses, because he had a bad feeling he'd passed the point of reason. And even though he'd never been in this position before, he strongly suspected that, while a woman could forgive a man for a lot, sleeping with her before true confessions wouldn't go over well.

I'm not lying to her. Exactly.

Good try. Every time Gabby started to open up about her mother's murder or anything related to it, he was viciously torn between not hurting her and wanting to push until her memories broke free.

He wasn't so different from the original investigators, he admitted, not liking the comparison but unable to deny it. He hoped he was more competent. Compassionate, too. He hadn't blown this by making love to a woman whose testimony he needed, but he'd come close. And he couldn't forget that those cops had been straight with her—they were police detectives interviewing her because of what she'd seen. Even a kid understood that.

Him, he was a police detective who was pretending his profession was incidental to his relationship with her. Had to be habit that had him jumping on her every time something slipped out. How many times had he apologized now?

Driving on autopilot, not so smart for anyone in law enforcement, Jack knew himself to be in deep trouble. He was seriously in danger of falling in love with a courageous, vulnerable, damaged woman who trusted him and shouldn't. A woman he'd been lying to since day one.

No, he should be glad she'd suddenly panicked and retreated into her room without inviting him to join her. Too bad his body still ached.

GABBY SHOULD HAVE been tired after Jack left—it wasn't as if she'd been sleeping well—but she wasn't. There was bound to be something on TV that could hold her attention. If not, the hotel offered a long list of current and older movies she could select from.

Latching on to the idea, she picked up the remote and started clicking through channels. She could watch hockey, football, basketball—hey, that game might actually be live—or curling. Gabby stayed on that channel for a few minutes. Men whisking brooms around on the ice held a certain fascination. Since she didn't understand what was going on, she clicked the channel button again. She lingered here and there, catching scenes from familiar movies and other ones from shows that didn't quite entice her to stick with them.

Suddenly, *Ghostbusters* popped up. Dan Aykroyd, Bill Murray and one of the other guys whose names she didn't remember were running out of a building, garbed in their ghost-hunting getups. Gabby's heart took a sickening thud. Her hand was shaking so much, it took several seconds for her to push another button. This one turned the TV off.

She stared at the dark screen as if it were a window behind which a monster had showed its face. Ridiculous, but she'd never been able to watch any of the *Ghostbusters* movies once she was old enough to appreciate them. Ric had had the original two on video and thought they were the best. He frequently had one or the other on when she wanted to watch something different, or was playing in the living room while he watched. She'd been way too young to appreciate the movies, but they were still embedded in her brain. She pictured her mother rolling her eyes and saying, "Not that again! For heaven's sake, turn it off!"

So why did the very idea of *Ghostbusters* disturb

her so much? And why hadn't she ever asked herself that question? She'd just…shied away.

It wasn't the actors, she was confident about that, or even the story lines. The whole idea was clever. And ghosts…she didn't believe in those. As awful as visiting the house had been, Mom hadn't been lingering.

So, what?

Confronting her disquiet directly for the first time, Gabby knew the answer almost instantly. It was the marshmallow man. Pulse racing, she opened her laptop case and went online, querying *Ghostbusters*. There he was, the eerily friendly-looking white monster striding down the street, towering over the people.

Just as he'd towered over her.

Teeth clenched tight, she closed the laptop. The Stay Puft Marshmallow Man had murdered her mother. No, of course not—but her childish mind had related the killer to the movie visual. Gabby closed her eyes. White, loose fabric, covering the head, too. Gloves, there must have been gloves, and foot coverings.

In her nightmare, blood had dripped from a white elbow.

Wow. It seemed clear as day suddenly. That made her wonder if she could be manufacturing a memory, but she knew she wasn't. And she finally understood why she'd immediately clicked away from any news coverage during the pandemic showing medical personnel and body recovery workers wearing protective suits. She'd been annoyed by her own squeamishness without questioning the reason for it.

Her nightmares had diminished as the years went on, and they had always varied. Sometimes, all she could recall was blood, or her mother's face or the smell of the dirty clothes forming the cocoon that saved her life. The memory of the puffy white getup had obviously lurked in her subconscious, but maybe it was the most recent nightmares that made it resurface.

Her first instinct was to call Jack. Gabby actually looked around for her phone before realizing how late it was. He might still be up…but, really, telling him could wait. It wasn't like she could describe the killer, or suddenly remembered her mother exclaiming, "John Smith, why are you here?" This memory was another piece to the picture, that was all.

It wasn't like Jack was investigating the crime, but she gathered he did work on homicides. He could surely make note of what she'd recalled, in case any other information ever surfaced. Although actually… in a way he *was* on the case, considering the possible attempts on her life. He was certainly determined to keep her alive, and the best way to do that was to identify her mother's murderer.

Or for her to fly back East and never visit Leclaire again, she supposed, oddly depressed by the idea. Ric would come visit her, she felt sure. Their relationship had come at least that far. But Jack…what if she never saw him again?

Oh, even thinking that was ridiculous. It wasn't

much over a week ago that they'd met. No surprise, he was still largely a mystery to her. He had a lot locked down tight, she suspected. Of course, he wasn't alone in that, but circumstances had forced her to reveal more of herself to him and to her brother than she ever had to anyone before.

And that probably explained why she was starting to remember the few horrific minutes that had changed her life forever.

"WELL, NEITHER OF my kids was the same age as Colleen," Annette Davis told Jack. A pleasant-looking, slim woman who appeared younger than her sixty-five years, she hadn't bothered dyeing her short dark hair, which was attractively streaked with silver.

He'd called ahead to ask if she had time to speak to him. While they were still on the porch, she pointed out the house where Colleen's parents had lived.

"They retired to Arizona." Leading the way into the living room of the nice rambler, she shook her head. "They were both killed in an awful head-on collision on the highway not that much later. Gabrielle would have been only two or three."

When she offered him a cup of coffee, he accepted. If he ever knew, he'd forgotten what had happened to Gabby's maternal grandparents. She hadn't mentioned them. Probably didn't remember them at all. Isabel, he seemed to recall Ric saying, was a sister to this grandmother who'd died so unexpectedly.

Gabby's family had suffered too much tragedy.

When Annette returned, he got her talking about

the family next-door and Colleen in particular. She was such a nice girl, of course, but he had the sense that Annette really meant it.

"A good Catholic girl," she added. "Our families belonged to the same church. Dolly and I served on the altar guild together, and put together dozens of potlucks over the years. My Matthew was an altar boy. Colleen sang in the choir her last few years of high school. She had the loveliest voice! I know she was active with the youth group, too. That girl never ran wild. Why, Russ and I had far more trouble with our daughter, although thank the good Lord she's happily married now, with three youngsters of her own."

"Colleen was an only child?"

"Yes, her parents doted on her, but she never acted as if she'd been spoiled."

It took her some effort, but she came up with the names of a couple of girls she remembered Colleen running around with. Both families had worshipped at St. Stephen's. Annette's still did.

"Of course Colleen brought her family there, too, and Raul continued to bring Ric." Sadness softened this nice woman's face. "Ric had his father buried in the churchyard, right next to his mother, but like so many young people, his attendance at services dropped off as time passed. I hope he makes his way back." Her expression brightened. "Has he married?"

"No." Jack didn't see how it would hurt to tell Annette about Gabby so he did. She grew teary at the idea of little Gabby home again.

"Having something so appalling happen to Colleen shocked everyone. Some of us who knew her still talk about it."

Jack had a thought. "I don't suppose the priest Colleen would have known is still at St. Stephen's."

"Oh, heavens no! We've had several changes. Father Ambrose was transferred… Oh, let me think." She pondered. "Matthew was in college, so Colleen would have been seventeen or eighteen, I think. We all missed him so much. His place was taken by Father Paul, who was also gone by the time Colleen died. We had Father Michael after that. He only retired a few years ago." Suddenly she blushed and pressed her hands to her cheeks. "I'm sure that was far more than you wanted to know! Gracious, you should have stopped me."

"No, I'm interested," he said, honestly. "A priest she trusted might be someone Colleen would go to if something was troubling her."

"That's true, although she wouldn't confess unless she felt she'd done something wrong."

He thought, but didn't say, *Maybe she did.* Maybe she had an affair. Maybe she'd just flirted when a good Catholic girl—or woman—shouldn't have. Slipped out at night without her parents knowing.

Except her killer didn't rape her, making it unlikely his motivation was sexual.

Having considered the possibility that the relationship between the killer and Colleen had dated back to her teenage years, he asked whether Annette knew if Colleen had had any boyfriends in high school.

"No boyfriends, as far as I know. I think Dolly

would have said. Colleen had this one stretch—I want to say her sophomore year—when she suddenly started wearing more makeup and, well, revealing clothes. You know. She and her mother had more than a few clashes, although I thought Dolly was overreacting." She shook her head. "It almost had to be a boy, don't you think? By that summer, she'd changed again. No more silliness. She seemed more mature after that. Quieter, more service oriented."

Or was she wary? Nervous around boys? Or had the desire to be of service to others been a way of atoning for what she'd viewed as a mistake? Could there have been a pregnancy and abortion? If she'd taken that route, she might well not have told her parents if she could have gotten away with it, but might have confessed to her priest.

Yet none of that explained the boy growing into a man who'd hated Colleen enough to murder her so brutally.

He could only hope what few school friends of Colleen's he'd been able to identify would be as helpful as this woman—and that Colleen had confided any problems she'd had then with boys. Or men, for that matter.

He'd been following other threads, but none that seemed very promising. Two men the original investigators had identified as friends or even just acquaintances of Raul and Colleen had caught Jack's attention. Both had the kind of job that required them to wear uniforms. One repaired washers and dryers for Sears. He'd serviced appliances twice at the Ortiz house in the year and a half before the murder. The other was then a security guard at a manufacturing plant in Leclaire.

The security guard especially interested him. The man had changed jobs several times in the years before the murder. The detectives who interviewed Royce Tilman had no way of knowing that he'd be accused of rape a couple of years after Colleen's death. He'd been arrested, but prosecutors didn't feel they had enough evidence to bring him to trial. Not surprisingly, he was fired from his job.

The only thing was, his wife had stuck by him, and they'd moved out of the area. They'd gone to Bellingham, in western Washington, and stayed there for ten years. Royce had been steadily employed for those years.

That's when Jack lost him. They had to have moved out of state. Monday he'd call the employer in Bellingham and find out if, when he was resigning, he'd told them where he was going.

Sitting in his vehicle, wishing the heat would crank up faster, Jack made another couple of phone calls in an attempt to locate Tilman. Both were futile.

Colleen's friends next, he decided, then a coworker from the year she'd worked as a nurse before her marriage.

CONVERSATION LAPSED BRIEFLY while Gabby and Jack dug into their entrées. Tonight was Thai again, starting with fried spring rolls, one of her favorite foods. So far, neither had said anything about that kiss.

After a few bites of her red curry, Gabby gathered her resolve and laid down her fork. "Something happened last night."

Jack's gaze acquired an intensity it hadn't had a second ago. "What?"

She told him about channel surfing, and how she'd happened on one of the *Ghostbusters* movies, then how it tied to her nightmare and ultimately to her memory.

"So that's why—" He shook his head.

"Why?"

"I've gathered you didn't see his face."

"I was looking at his back when he killed Mom." How calm she sounded. "The only thing is..." Oh, why say this?

He waited with his usual patience, until she finally admitted, "Lately, a couple of times in nightmares he's suddenly looked at me. I'm not...really seeing a face, but..." She shook herself. "It's probably symbolic of my fear that he'd see me."

"Probably." Jack said that more thoughtfully than she liked, but he must have learned to be dispassionate on the job. Then he studied her face, the lines deepening on his. "Why don't we talk about something else until we're done eating. Then...will you tell me everything you do remember? Maybe we can put it together into something that makes sense."

Her heart tripped a few times. She told herself gathering her courage to tell him the one recollection wasn't the same as immersing herself in the real nightmare. Plus, she thought she was ready. She appreciated the kindness she heard in his voice and the efforts he'd made to protect her, and by good fortune, he was a detective.

Gabby nodded. "Okay."

He did shift the conversation, asking whether her aunt had been a churchgoer, saying his mom had dragged him and his sister to church—in their case, Presbyterian—every Sunday, but after the divorce, his attendance had lapsed along with his father's.

Aunt Isabel had been Catholic as well, but Gabby hadn't stayed faithful any more than he had.

"I suppose it's hard to believe, doing the job you do," she commented.

He grimaced. "It is. Not impossible, but when you see something really bad, you have to ask why. When you don't get an answer—" He lifted one shoulder.

"Yet our instinct when we're scared is to pray."

"Because we want to be bailed out. Is that real faith?"

They argued amicably about the unanswerable question, then talked about friends who'd made drastically different life choices than they had. Once again, Gabby thought how different her conversations with Jack were than what she was used to on dates.

After their plates had been removed and they were sipping coffee, he said, "Would you consider inviting me to your room to talk? Or coming back to my place?" His expression was grave, and she knew he wasn't thinking about sex.

She nodded. "The hotel is closer."

"Okay."

In fact, they'd walked the several blocks to the restaurant, Jack staying on the curbside, his gaze constantly roving. He'd been so obviously in bodyguard mode, she hadn't even tried to start a conversation.

It was the same as they walked back to the hotel. Plenty of people were still out and about, which meant he frequently put a hand on her back and edged her out of the way of other pedestrians. She remembered what Ric said about Jack having eyes in the back of his head, and that had never seemed more true than tonight. He knew when people approached or came out of open doorways, even behind them, and screened her with his body when cars passed.

The reminder that there was a good reason for him to be so cautious wasn't exactly soothing, even if she was grateful for it. Then there was her agreement to let him interview her in a way that hadn't happened since her traumatic experiences as a little girl. By the time they passed through the hotel lobby and got into an elevator, Gabby felt sure a doctor reading her blood pressure right now would insist on medication.

But during that silent ride up in the elevator, she stiffened her spine enough to add that extra half inch to her height, and determined that she was going through with this. The time was right, and this man was right.

Chapter Eleven

He couldn't believe this was actually happening. He had to caution himself that she might not remember anything significant.

Jack moved restlessly around her room, peered into the bathroom to ensure it was empty and closed the drapes while Gabby waited, stock-still, in the middle of the room. She still clutched her handbag. Only her head turned to allow her to watch him.

He'd expected her to be nervous, but scared to death wouldn't help.

"Hey." He took the bag from her hand and dropped it on a table. Then he summoned a wicked grin, not hard considering his exhilaration. "You need to get comfortable before we start our session. I'd suggest you change clothes, preferably into something less confining. Say, a lacy negligee. Then you can stretch out on my couch." He waggled his eyebrows as he nodded toward the queen-size bed.

That broke the spell. She shook her head, rolled her eyes and laughed, if huskily. "Forget the couch.

I do think I'll change clothes, though, if you don't mind waiting."

"Not at all." He planted himself in one of the room's pair of easy chairs. Waiting five minutes was no problem; he'd already waited fifteen years or more for this opportunity. Longer than that, of course, if he were to include the years before he started college with a single goal: arresting the man he'd blamed for shattering his father's life.

Gabby grabbed a few things from her suitcase that lay open on a luggage rack in the closet, then disappeared into the bathroom.

His mood strange, Jack thought about the most recent call with his father. Had he blinded himself all these years to the truth, that his parents' divorce had little to do with the brief police interest in Dad? That while there were things his mother had always refused to tell him, his father was hiding plenty, too?

Gabby had become more of a priority than he'd expected, too, and he truly believed that she needed to know her mother's killer was behind bars, that she herself would be safe. She needed to let go of guilt, to be able to release those horrific memories so they were out in the open instead of taunting her from the shadows.

The toilet flushed behind the closed bathroom door, and a moment later water ran.

Damn. Should he tell her now that he was already deep into a cold case investigation of her mother's murder?

But enough of his exhilaration lingered to make

him balk. No, that wasn't all of it—but in telling her, he'd be taking a significant risk that she'd refuse to talk to him. She'd be mad, he felt confident of that. If she decided not to trust him...

He swore under his breath.

If he went ahead with this, he was very possibly ruling out any chance that she'd ever trust him again. He could be throwing away any hope of getting this woman who'd made him feel so much, so fast, into bed. But he'd be a fool to let this chance go by, he told himself grimly. If she couldn't understand why he'd made the decisions he'd had, then what kind of relationship would it be, anyway?

The bathroom door opened and she appeared, expression tentative. His body clenched at the sight of her in pajamas, even if they were the furthest thing from sexy. Still, beneath those flannel pants and thin knit T-shirt, she had to be naked. The movement of her generous breasts beneath that top as she walked toward him had his fingers flexing.

Too quick, she was past him and on the bed. Sitting back against the pile of pillows at the headboard, legs crossed, she clutched a pillow from the other side of the bed to herself, hiding her magnificent breasts.

He had to order himself to breathe. It was just as well she'd assumed such an obviously defensive posture. She wasn't trying to be seductive. In fact, between the pretzel she'd formed with her entwined legs and the way she hugged that pillow to herself, he was unpleasantly reminded of the little girl whose timid voice he'd heard on those damn tapes.

He forced a grin. "You followed my advice."

"It…seemed to make sense."

After a brief hesitation, Jack crossed the room and gestured toward a spot at the foot of the bed. "Okay if I sit there?"

"What? Oh, sure."

The mattress shifted under his weight, but he was a safe distance from her. "How do you want to do this?" he asked her. "I'll ask questions if you want, or you can close your eyes and tell me what you remember in order. Or what your nightmares are suggesting you remember."

Her beautiful eyes met his. "I…that might be best."

He pressed the heel of his hand against his breastbone in hopes of easing the unexpected ache.

"Well," she said. "Um, here goes."

INSTEAD OF CLOSING her eyes, she lowered her gaze to be sure she wasn't sucked into Jack's force field. For the first time in a very long while, she dragged herself back to that morning.

"My mother let me run through the sprinkler," Gabby told him. "She said I had to turn off the water before I came in, so I did. Only, I didn't take a towel outside, so when I came in I was dripping."

Dripping. Oh, God.

She corrected herself hastily. "I left wet footprints. Mom said to go to the laundry room and strip. There'd be towels in the dirty clothes basket I could use to dry myself before I went upstairs to change."

Beginning before the intruder appeared seemed

to be helping. It was as if, once the reel had started, it didn't stop running. "That's where I was, when I heard the back door open again. Mommy said, 'Ric? Is that you?' Then...then..." Gabby swallowed. "She said, 'What are *you* doing here?'"

When she froze up, Jack asked gently, "Could you see him?"

"Uh-uh. Only Mommy." Vaguely, she knew how childish she sounded, but that's who was telling this story: the little girl she'd been. "She looked scared, like the time I crossed the street when I wasn't supposed to, and for a minute she didn't see me in the yard." She frowned. "I think that's when I crouched down behind the laundry basket. Mommy being scared made me want to hide."

"Good call." Jack's soft murmur barely touched her.

"Mommy backed up until she bumped into the island in the kitchen." Now Gabby closed her eyes as she strained to *see*. "She sort of shuffled sideways, like she was trying to go around it."

"How are you seeing this?"

"I'm peeking over the top of the laundry basket. She's yelling at him. I don't know what she's saying." She squeezed her eyes shut even harder, trying to pull herself back from *being* the child again. Failing. "Then he's in the way. All I can see is his back, but he's like the scary monster in *Ghostbusters*. He's so big! And...and he has something in his hand. Mommy is yelling about how she won't tell, she promises, and he says, 'Now I know you won't.'"

Lord. She was shaking, her teeth chattering, just like they probably were then. He could so easily have heard. The mattress compressed a little, and somehow she knew Jack had moved even before he wrapped an arm around her.

That warmth helped settle her. *It's all over. I'm not that little girl anymore. I never will be again.*

"She kept screaming," Gabby said dully, "and he yelled, 'You ruined my life.' Over and over. He lifted his arm and brought it down, over and over. Blood sprayed. I didn't know that's what it was, I just saw red. Red ran all over the floor. In my dream, it looked like veins in the human body, except it was blood that *wasn't* in a human body anymore. I…got so scared I pulled a pile of dirty sheets over me." Green sheets, which meant they were from Ric's bed. How odd. If someone had asked, she wouldn't have been able to tell them. "But it got quiet, so I peeked. My mother was just lying there, but her face was *wrong*, like she smashed it in spaghetti sauce. I couldn't really see *him*, but I knew he was still there. I think he turned on the water in the kitchen sink. I don't know what he was doing." She sounded robotic now, not like child Gabby or adult Gabby. "Then…he walked toward me. He had a full plastic trash bag in his arms. I had this moment of wondering if he was taking the garbage out. That was supposed to be Ric's job."

Abruptly, she realized she was wheezing. The safe distance wasn't working anymore. She pressed her face into Jack's chest and felt him lay his cheek on her head. He was saying something that sounded urgent, but she couldn't make it out.

Horror held her in a terrible grip. "He looked right at me. I never moved, and...and he walked by. That's when he was dressed in blue."

"Jeans?"

She did hear that. "No. I think they were like uniform pants. Navy blue. His shoes were black and shiny. Dad used to let me help shine his. These were like that."

"Bigger than your dad's?"

After a minute, she said, "Yes. Lots bigger."

"Did he go out the back door?"

"I don't know," she had to say again. "I guess he must have. I just...made myself small, wrapped in sheets and thought, *He can't see me. He can't.*"

"All right." Jack sounded angry. "That's enough, Gabby. Do you hear me?" He pushed her away enough to lift her chin with one of his hands. "No more."

"He can't see me," she whispered. "He can't."

"No. Damn it, he didn't see you!"

If he had, she'd be dead. Gabby had always known that.

But I *must have seen him,* she understood in horror. And *that's* why he wanted her dead.

Panting, she stared at Jack. "What if I told the police that I saw him look right at me? If I did—"

"You didn't," he said sharply. "Anyway, how would he know what you told them?"

"But if I didn't, why did he try to kill me back

then?" she begged. "And why does he still think he has to kill me?"

"Because there's a risk you did see him. He must have heard there was a child witness. Even if you didn't see his face," Jack's voice slowed, "there might have been something else about him that would point investigators his way."

"Like him wearing blue."

"Yes, but that wasn't as much help as it could have been, because blue uniforms are fairly common in the service industry, and he might have happened to wear blue chinos with a chambray shirt."

"No."

He tipped his head. "No?"

Gabby scrambled. *Why did I say that?* Because… she could picture that much. "Chambray is usually a lighter shade of blue. I think his pants and shirt matched exactly."

"So we're back to a uniform. You said navy blue."

She nodded cautiously. "Is that the color of your dad's uniform?"

His mouth compressed and he nodded.

"Did he wear shiny black shoes?"

Jack stared at her for a long moment. "No. Work boots. He had to protect his feet from dropping something heavy on them. Shiny sounds like…"

"Dress shoes," she supplied. "Only…" She tried really hard to arrow in on that one specific detail. "I don't know," she said finally. "I can't quite see it."

His expression became calculating in a way that bothered her, but what had she expected? He was a cop. What a coup it would be for him if he could actually arrest her mother's murderer.

"He looked right at you."

She bit her lip. "At the pile of dirty clothes in front of the washer."

"If you know that, you must have seen his face."

Inexplicable panic rose in her. "I didn't really. I don't remember."

"Okay, sweetheart." His hands swept up and down her nearly bare arms. Did she actually have goose bumps? "Let's try it another way. Did he have a beard?"

"No." *How do I know that, if I didn't see his face?* But she was sure. Nobody in the neighborhood had a beard. A few of father's friends had moustaches. She'd have noticed anything like that.

"Was he blond?"

"I don't know."

"Dark haired?"

She shook her head and kept shaking it.

"Isn't hair color one of the first identifiers we notice about people?"

She opened her mouth to say, *I don't know,* but shut it.

"Was his face blurry?"

"Blurry?" And then she got it. "Like in movies when a bank robber wears pantyhose over his head."

"Right."

"I don't think so. I just think his head sort of turned toward me but I couldn't see that much of his face."

"Because your peephole was so small?"

"No…yes." Then words came from her mouth before she could analyze them. "He had on a hat."

The triumph on Jack's face disturbed her as much as the way he kept rapping out questions. Fast, inexorable. "A fedora?"

"You mean, like the man on the hotel tape wore?"

"Yeah."

Gabby frowned. "I don't think so."

"But it had a brim to shadow his face."

She nodded, because it must have.

"Baseball cap?"

She didn't even know why she hesitated, but that didn't seem quite right. The trouble was, her four-year-old self thought only *hat*. At that age, she had no idea what a fedora was or how to describe it, never mind a newsboy cap or—

Her mind shut down. All she could see was the glint of eyes beneath a brim. When she shook her head, Jack studied her, then tucked her close to his body again.

"It'll come to you," he said softly.

"I wish I could remember everything *now*. Get it over with." Something an awful lot like grief seized her in sharp teeth. This was twenty-five years too late, but she'd just seen her mother murdered again, and this time she'd understood what she was seeing.

She grabbed a handful of the Jack's collar and pressed her face harder into that solid chest. *I won't cry, I won't cry.* But of course she did. Not long, but when her body quit shaking, she felt drained, empty.

She hadn't known Jack had shifted her over on the

bed and now sat where she'd been, his back against
the cushioned headboard, his legs stretched out. Both
of her arms wrapped his torso, and now she had his
sweater in back squeezed in a fist.

"Your sweater is cashmere, isn't it?" she mumbled
after a minute.

"Ah—I don't know. It was a Christmas present
from my mother a few years back. I don't wear it very
often because it has to be dry-cleaned, but I wanted
to impress you. Did it?"

She gurgled a laugh. "Yes, except now I've cried
all over it. There's probably a little snot mixed in."

His chest shook with a husky laugh. "That's what
dry cleaners are for."

She kept lying against him, feeling no urgency to
move. In fact, she drifted, thinking about, oh, small,
immediate things. Sensations and textures. The deep
blue of the cashmere was perfect with Jack's eyes. His
mother had good taste, she thought dreamily. It was
incredibly soft beneath her cheek, too.

Blue—no, she didn't want to think about colors
anymore, except Jack did have beautiful eyes. After
a bit, she began to wish the layer of cashmere wasn't
between her and his broad, powerful chest. She could
see brown hair curling at the neck opening. She could
lift herself a little bit and kiss him there, on that hol-
low at the base of his throat.

Somehow, Gabby wasn't nearly as relaxed as she'd
been. She was tempted to squirm even closer than she
already was. She could pretend she was just trying to
get more comfortable...

He hadn't moved in a couple of minutes, she realized suddenly. She'd swear his heartbeat had picked up. Was he breathing at all? She stole a peek and that's when she saw a ridge beneath the zipper placket of his chinos.

This was why she'd resisted inviting him into her room.

DAMN, HE'D HOPED she wouldn't look down. This was the worst of times for him to get so obviously aroused. Gabby had just been through another traumatic experience, had cried on him and was pulling herself together. And him? He couldn't stop thinking about the curvaceous body he held in his arms.

Then a small, husky voice said, "Will you make love with me?"

Jack froze. Did she mean that? He gritted his teeth as his need for her surged. His brain didn't seem to want to work. He was already kneading her hip, his other hand making circles on her belly, easing upward toward her breasts.

"You're sure?" His voice had gone guttural.

"Yes." Gabby tipped her face up. Her even white teeth nibbled on her full lower lip. "I don't want to be a coward anymore."

With a groan, he twisted so that he could kiss her. He had her flat on her back in seconds, his body half covering hers. Her breast overflowed his hand, just firm enough to make him think of ripe fruit. The taut bud pressed against his palm. He wanted to see her, all of her, which meant backing off and stripping her, but from the moment he had set eyes on her, he'd also wanted to free her glossy black hair from the braid. It wouldn't hurt if he could rip his own clothes off, too. At least he had a condom; he'd carried a couple around since meeting her.

She tried to tangle her fingers in his hair, but it was too short to cooperate. He didn't mind her pulling it.

Feeling her struggle beneath him, he dragged his mouth from hers, only to realize she was trying to tug his sweater off. He cooperated and yanked the T-shirt over her head while they were at it. Then, when he saw the ripe swell of her breasts and the taut nipples, he lost it.

What reason he'd retained went AWOL. Forget his shirt, he was already suckling one breast while he reached beneath the elastic waistband of her pajama pants and slid his fingers along the slick passage between her folds. Whimpering, she arched upward, lifting her breast to his mouth, her fingernails biting into his shoulders.

He kissed and suckled her breasts, returning every few minutes to her mouth. There was so much he wanted to do to her, with her, but he became increasingly desperate.

When he yanked down her pants, she squeezed him through the fabric of his trousers. His hips responded eagerly even as he struggled to get her naked. Once she became determined enough to start unzipping his slacks, Jack took over. Boots first, socks, then pants. *No, don't toss them. Have to keep my wallet.* He pulled out the two packets and had no idea what became of his wallet after that. Getting the condom on while he kissed her was a challenge. Then he explored her slick flesh with his fingers, said, "I need you," and parted her thighs.

"Yes. Please. Please, please," she chanted as he found her entrance and forged his way inside, going deep.

For one moment, suspended above her, he drank in the sight of her gorgeous face, lips parted, dazed green-gold eyes focused on his. And then he pulled back, drove deep again, and kept doing it as she pushed to meet every thrust, kept saying his name, wrapped one leg over his hip while the other foot stayed planted on the bed to give her leverage. It was madness, it was pleasure, it was frighteningly new. When her convulsions started and she made a sound he'd never forget, Jack let himself go.

Chapter Twelve

Gabby felt drunk, but in a good way. It was like becoming weightless at the same time as she reveled in *his* weight on her. When he stirred, her arms tightened. She didn't want to let him go.

"I'm crushing you," he mumbled.

"Uh-uh."

Of course, superior muscle mass meant he had his way. She grumbled after he rolled off until he rearranged her to sprawl half-atop him. With her head on that wide, powerful shoulder, she could study the curly hair on his chest, brown to match the hair on his head. She turned her head enough to kiss his taut, salty skin before settling down dreamily. Either she was hearing her own heartbeat, or that was his. Or maybe they'd synced to beat in time. Could that happen?

She drifted, her entire body tingling. Her toes kept curling. Why had she bothered resisting Jack? But she knew the answer, she'd already told him. They hadn't known each other much more than a week. Physical risks didn't scare her as much as emotional ones. She'd lost too many people in her life already and had shaped her decisions to avoid any more losses on that scale.

Right now, she felt too good to stiffen even as darkness began to tinge her thoughts.

He lifted his head from the pillow, distracting her, and gave her the single, sexiest smile she'd ever seen. "Your hair."

"What?"

The hand that had been stroking her back lifted her braid. The next thing she knew, he'd peeled off the elastic and was concentrating on freeing her hair from the tight confinement. Once the annoyingly thick black mass fell loose over her back and face and shoulders, he told her how beautiful it was as he ran his fingers through the waves left from the braid. The intense concentration and happiness on his face made her glow inside.

But amazing as she felt physically, awareness of her internal bruises awakened. Had she really remembered everything for all these years?

Yes and no, she decided. More memories had been waiting for her to call them up than she'd guessed, but her recent nightmares and coming home to Leclaire, even seeing the house, had stirred the bits and pieces she'd been missing. On a guilty pang, she wondered if she'd been able to tell this much to detectives at the time, would they have been able to find her mother's murderer?

She'd been too young to think like that. It had been days before she'd managed more than a few hysterical words. She'd curled her body as tight as she could make it most of the time, usually in bed under her covers just as she had beneath those sheets. *He can't see me. He can't.* She'd secretly started sucking her thumb at night, when no one would see her. Her father had had to haul her out for meals and when he couldn't stand knowing that's all she was doing.

The police… She couldn't remember their exact questions, but a few stuck out. The detectives had jumped around, as if they were trying to trick her into answering instead of patiently coaxing a child's narrative. They'd scared her, all three of those men. They weren't dressed like the other people at the police station, but she could see their badges and guns and hear their impatience.

Truthfully, Gabby didn't remember what she *had* told them. Obviously, that the killer had worn what looked like a blue uniform when he walked out, or else Jack's father wouldn't have been a suspect. Otherwise, she suspected she'd been huddling inside herself even when she was in a conference room or sitting on a chair in the hotel room being interviewed.

Why hadn't she told anyone the killer had been puffy and white when he appeared? Was she afraid it sounded too silly to say, "He was the marshmallow man"?

Her happy glow diminished further when she thought about Jack's relentless string of questions. *Was he blond? Did he have a beard? Blurry? Baseball cap?* And the hardness in his voice when he said, *If you know that, you must have seen his face.*

He's a cop, she reminded herself. Jumping in to question a witness must be second nature to him. Which meant she had been a witness in his mind until they finished and he regained awareness of her as a woman. He was a far more skilled interviewer than the ones who'd terrified her as a child, able to soften his tone and encourage her when that was what she needed, ask that sharp question when he sensed the answer was surfacing in her head.

And he hadn't backed off when she became distressed.

If you know that, you must have seen his face.

Something he'd said had jarred her at the time. Gabby fought to separate it from all the rest. It didn't help that she was still reveling in cuddling with him, bare skin to bare skin, or relishing the sensations as his hands continued to wander from one sensitive spot to another. She could easily become aroused again if she weren't also bugged by what had come before.

Then it slipped into place. She'd been near frantic when she said, *What if I told the police that I saw him look right at me? If I did—*

And he said, *You didn't.*

How did he know she hadn't? Did he know more than usual about the investigation just because it had involved his father? Or had he gone digging when he first joined the police force, or more recently when the odd things started happening after she arrived in Leclaire? If so, why hadn't he told her? Wouldn't it have made sense for him to say, "I went looking for some background, and here are some things I learned"?

Yes.

Earlier, there'd been another thing. She'd explained about the marshmallow man, and Jack had said, *So that's why—*, then broken off.

He claimed he was thinking that's why she hadn't seen the killer's face, but he already knew she had seen the man when he wasn't wearing what she now guessed was a Tyvek suit.

So what had he meant?

JACK WAS REELING from a combination of the best sex of his life and Gabby's extraordinarily detailed testimony about her mother's murder. If the then-detectives hadn't been such fools, they might have gotten somewhere. He'd known some of the answers were in her head, but he was still stunned at how she'd woven the child's view with details her nightmares had helped her unlock. No, she hadn't identified the killer, but he had a feeling there was more yet lurking in her head. Even if she couldn't describe the man's face, she'd seen it. If she met up with him now, would her subconscious know him?

And that hat. He bet her adult self was already thinking, *Hmm. A four-year-old wouldn't know what kind of hat he wore, but I do.*

Jack hoped like hell that would happen, because he had a bad feeling about the hat, the navy blue uniform, the shiny black shoes that weren't typical dress shoes. Say they were more substantial, had a thicker sole that allowed for action.

He'd worn a uniform like that for seven years before he'd been promoted. There were plenty of workers in other professions that used protective suits, but they'd be readily available to a law enforcement officer.

"You…seem really invested in finding out what I remembered," she said suddenly.

Oh, hell. He turned his head on the pillow, but couldn't see her face well enough to read it.

"I'm worried about you," he said after a minute.

"Are you?"

He jackknifed to a sitting position, which sent her tumbling off him and scrambling to sit up herself. Worse yet, she clutched the sheet and bedspread to cover herself. "What does that mean? You don't think I give a damn if a cold-blooded killer runs you down on an icy street or murders you in your hotel room?"

She laid a hand on his arm and squeezed. "That's not true. I know you do. You wouldn't be in law enforcement if you didn't care. That…has to be a big part of your personality."

"You're saying I don't care about you personally."

This, when he'd realized just tonight what had been happening to him since he'd gotten to know her. His priorities had done more than shift. They'd tumbled on end.

His father didn't need him to be able to proclaim to the world, *See? You were wrong to suspect him for a second!* Even if Colleen Ortiz's murder had impacted his parents' relationship, they'd both moved on. He alone had stayed fixated on a single goal: arresting her killer. He still wanted to accomplish that, but only for Gabby. To give her answers, to free her from her fears, to stop a murderous bastard from killing *her*.

What he cared most about now was Gabby.

"I've gotten a funny feeling about you a few times." She sounded unnervingly thoughtful, but he heard the underlying distress, too.

He could keep lying to her. Tell her he'd gone digging in the files because of what had been happening to her and at the house. She'd believe him. But what if they had a chance at a future together? What if she ever found out the truth?

And could he go on with this kind of lie between them?

No. He'd known all along that he couldn't, that it would come to this. What he had to do was make her understand that she'd been an abstraction before he met her, but that everything had changed since.

Jack let out a long breath. "I've told you my father was a suspect."

Wary eyes watched him.

"What I didn't say is that a lot of people kept suspecting he really had killed your mother. The police couldn't prove he'd done it…but he was the only suspect they'd come up with. If there's smoke, there has to be fire, right?"

Gabby still didn't say anything.

"Things changed then between my parents. I still don't know if Mom believed for a minute that Dad would do something like that, or if she was embarrassed because she knew what other people were thinking, or—"

Wandering from the point.

"I grew up thinking my family would have stayed together if the cops had arrested the killer, that I wouldn't have lost my mother and sister, that Dad wouldn't have finally had to move away, too. I became a cop so *I* could arrest that monster."

"That's why you stayed in Leclaire," she said slowly. "Why you became a detective."

"Yeah. The job…suits me," he admitted. "It's not like I've been hunting your mother's killer night and day since I joined the force."

Even more slowly, she said, "Just since I came back to town."

True confessions. Damn. He wished he'd gotten dressed before they started this. What would she think if he reached for his pants?

"When I made detective," he said, "I read about your mom's murder, what I could without having to get permission. The only solid tie I had to those days was Ric, but we'd mostly gone our own ways. I wanted to keep in touch, so I changed health clubs so I'd run into him now and again."

"He doesn't know that, I assume."

"No."

Jack had the unnerving feeling she was watching him the way she might a student taking a test whom she suspected of cheating.

"He told you about my visit."

"He did. We'd…talked about you now and again." He moved his shoulders uncomfortably. "Because we had a history. He…kept me up to date."

"That's why you came to dinner that first evening. Ric and I had already quarreled and you didn't want me to get away."

"It was more complicated than that."

She let out a disbelieving laugh. "Sure it was. That's why you asked me out the next evening, and every time since then. If I hadn't asked you to make love to me—no, to have sex with me—we wouldn't be in this bed right now, would we? I suppose you have enough sense of honor to think it was wrong to go quite this far to wring an interview out of me." Her voice could have etched glass.

"You have to know I was attracted to you from the beginning." He sounded as desperate as he felt. "I knew I had to tell you the truth before I made love to you or talked about where we can take this relationship. Yes, I wanted your trust, but I'd never have—"

"And yet you did." The pain in her eyes ripped him open. "I suppose I should give you some credit. Your goal was estimable. But you could have done this entirely differently. The irony is that I hoped to recover my memories when I came home. Once I worked through my instinctive panic, I'd have been glad to talk to you. Instead, you've left me feeling dirty and ashamed that I was too stupid to realize how obvious you were. Of course I'm the most beautiful woman ever, and you can't stay away." Her laugh was razor sharp. "Congratulations. You're good at your job. I have nothing more to contribute, so I'm asking you to go now."

"Gabby, damn it, listen to me! I shouldn't have let it get this far, but the way I feel about you is tangled up with my...quest." There was that damn word again. "Ric kept saying you refused to even talk about it, and I told myself you needed your mother's murder to be solved, too, that it had to have haunted you—"

She shook her head hard. Once. "Get out. I'll call the front desk if you don't leave right now."

"I know this is too soon, but I've been falling in love with you."

This laugh was worse. He didn't know why he wasn't bleeding. Jack managed to say, "I'm sorry."

In shock, he located his clothes and wallet. He got dressed, shoved his feet in his boots and looked around for his coat. At last he turned to face her and had the horrifying realization that she was holding herself together the same way she probably had as a child.

And *he'd* done this to her.

"I'll call you tomorrow," he said hoarsely.

"I won't answer. I never want to see you again."

This was worse than he'd expected, yet he couldn't blame her. After a moment, Jack nodded and left.

GABBY DIDN'T CRY. This felt too huge, too devastating. She'd have to tell Ric, but not tonight.

Tonight... Oh, God, she didn't know how she could bear all of this slamming her at the same time. The spray of blood, the ruin of her mother's face, the certainty that *he* had turned his head and looked right at her. Discovering how much she did remember caused guilt that she'd never told, that as an adult she'd been so determined to block it all to save herself from crippling memories.

And now Jack. It had happened ridiculously fast, but she'd been drawn to him at first sight, and liked all the complexities of his personality that she'd since discovered. Jack had slipped through her defenses, letting her see the boy he'd been, shattered by his parents' inexplicable divorce. He'd talked about his relationship with his father. Even about his job, the satisfactions, the frustrations, the need to learn to harden himself, in a sense, from the never-ending tragedy.

And he'd been lying to her—no, not just to her, to her and Ric—about why he wanted to spend time with them. He'd been deftly working her to the point where she'd spill all. She was furious, thinking of the several times he'd apologized for upsetting her with a question, or when he seemed angry at Ric for being so clueless about how seeing the weirdly unchanged house would affect her.

All a pretense, or at least, all carefully planned. She hated knowing how credulous she'd been, turning to him, trusting him, even going so far as having the passing thought that she might explore the job market around Spokane.

A raw sound escaped her as she remembered seeing Jack and Ric walking toward her that first night, at the Italian restaurant. Jack locking on to her like a heat-seeking missile, never looking away, traversing the crowded room with confident strides.

Oh, by the way, he was a cop. He'd seemed almost abashed when telling her he thought his choice of career had been influenced by her mother's murder. In retrospect, that was funny.

Well, yeah, he was a detective working major crimes—read *murder*—and he had a way of directing conversation back to the subject of Mom's murder even when she wanted to shy away.

He hadn't even been subtle, she thought now, feeling like a fool.

She'd had boyfriends, even a few semiserious relationships when she was in her early twenties and still pretending to be normal, but none had left her as devastated as she was now. She was tempted to grab her laptop and book a flight out of here tomorrow morning, but knew she had to talk to Ric first. Maybe get together with him again, let him drive her to the airport for a last hug.

It suddenly occurred to her that the day after tomorrow was Thanksgiving. She and Ric hadn't even talked about celebrating together, probably because the only place they could have cooked was his kitchen.

Or Jack's.

I've been falling in love with you.

Too bad that was as believable as just about everything else Jack had said to her.

THIS WAS REALLY bad timing to be summoned to Sergeant Rutkowski's office and find the police chief there, too.

Keeping his expression neutral with an effort, Jack said, "Sergeant. Chief. Can I do something for you?"

Rutkowski waved him to a seat. Jack felt like a sulky teenager summoned to the principal's office, especially since Chief Keller half sat on one end of the sergeant's desk. He appeared relaxed while also keeping a height advantage.

Jack sat, his back to a window with closed blinds that blocked the view into the squad room. He wondered if they were seeing the same death's head he had in his bathroom mirror a couple of hours ago.

"The chief dropped by to talk about something else, but your investigation into the Ortiz murder came up. You haven't given me much in the way of updates to pass on," Rutkowski pointed out. A big, bulky man with the homely face of a former boxer— although Jack had never heard he really had been— the sergeant was currently scowling. Best way to annoy him was to fail to keep him current on an investigation.

Chief Keller's expression was more curious than irritated, but Jack didn't know him well enough to guess whether that meant anything or not. Like the sergeant, Keller was a brawny man, any softening in his muscles disguised by well-cut suits. Handsome instead of homely, Keller had silver at his temples and scattered in his dark hair that helped give him a seemingly natural air of authority.

Dodging the necessity of really laying out what he'd learned, Jack still hadn't figured out what to say, and what to keep to himself. The memories Gabby had shared yesterday left him even unhappier.

Sergeant Roger Rutkowski and Police Chief Dean Keller were close to the age Colleen Ortiz would have been if she were still alive. Rutkowski had graduated from high school here in Leclaire, Keller attending for a couple of years, too, until his parents moved him to a military-style, regimented boarding school back East somewhere. In those days, there'd been only the one high school in town, so Colleen had very likely known or at least recognized either or both of Jack's bosses. Rutkowski had been raised Catholic, too, although his family had attended Assumption Catholic Church rather than St. Stephen's. Both men had been patrol officers when Gabby's mother was killed.

Both would have worn navy blue uniforms and kept the regulation black shoes shiny. That uniform included a hat.

Gabby hadn't mentioned seeing a holstered weapon or a shield—but the bulging plastic bag containing the bloody protective suit, gloves and separate shoe coverings, if there'd been any, as well as the knife, could well have hidden a badge and name on the chest pocket, and a gun and other accoutrements worn on the standard, heavy-duty black belt.

The Leclaire Police Department wasn't huge. Other men had also spent their entire careers with LPD. Jack hadn't yet had a chance to work his way through the entire police force, but the ones he'd taken a look at didn't jibe with the security camera footage of the man trying to get into Gabby's hotel room. Either of these two men might.

Of course, even if the killer was a police officer at the time, he might no longer be, or had moved on to a different law enforcement agency. Reason said he could have been a cop with another agency here in the Spokane area—but the navy blue uniform ruled out the City of Spokane PD and the county sheriff's department. State patrol officers wore blue, but not a shade Jack would call navy. And how likely was it that a state trooper assigned to this region at the time of the murder would have had any history with a local woman? He'd pursue that possibility only if he came up short on his current avenues of investigation.

Jack had begun tracking, with so-so success, a few men who'd been with LPD then but had left in the intervening years. In most cases, finding a photo was enough to rule them out. He wasn't wasting a lot of time on the ones who hadn't stayed in town, because one of the things bothering him from the beginning was the rapid reaction to Gabby's return to town. He still couldn't rule out the killer having been a neighbor, a school principal, an old family friend—any of the people Ric had told about her upcoming visit.

Both Rutkowski and Chief Keller had known about her from the moment Jack asked permission to reopen the case.

The sergeant's scowl was deepening, and even Chief Keller was starting to look annoyed at Jack's prolonged silence.

"I've had several meetings with Ms. Ortiz," he

said. "She's been reluctant to revisit those memories, as you can imagine. I didn't want to push too hard or too fast."

"Have you learned anything new?" Sergeant Rutkowski demanded.

"Yes. I know now that the killer initially wore what she described as a 'puffy' white one-piece coverall with a hood. Once he'd killed Colleen Ortiz, he stripped off the suit, used the kitchen sink briefly—you may recall that trace amounts of blood were found in it—then left carrying a plastic trash bag that presumably held the blood-soaked garments. That's when Gabrielle saw him wearing all blue."

Both men stared at him. It was the chief who said finally, "That's pretty specific. I assume you got more than that."

He said reluctantly, "Yeah, I did."

Chapter Thirteen

He'd just lied to his commanding officers, if mostly by omission.

Jack walked back to his desk, opened his laptop and pretended to become immersed in what he'd been working on before being summoned by the sergeant.

He had told them both that the killer had yelled, "You ruined my life!"

To which Chief Keller had nodded. "I vaguely recall her saying the murderer said his victim had ruined something. 'His life' doesn't necessarily enlarge on that. It still could imply Mrs. Ortiz had broken up his marriage, or…" He obviously groped for a second option.

"Had told his family something that meant they cut him off," suggested Rutkowski. "Or he lost a job because of her." He frowned. "Did she work out of the home?"

Jack shook his head. "She had an LPN certificate and was employed as a nurse for a year and a half before she got married. Stayed home after that. She might have intended to go back to work once the kids were both in school. I don't know."

"Working as a nurse, she could have learned something about him that he needed kept private," Keller pointed out. "Like the guy had syphilis, which meant he'd cheated on his wife—"

Jack was shaking his head before the chief could finish. "Colleen's job was in a nursing home."

They threw around more ideas. Once, the chief looked him in the eye and asked directly whether he had anything else new to add to the picture, and that's when he'd flat out lied. He not only said no, he didn't tell them everything Gabby had shared: that she'd also heard her mother saying she'd never tell, or the killer responding with, "Now you won't."

He left out the shiny black shoes, the hat and the disturbing fact that the killer had looked straight at Gabby on his way out.

That Keller had remembered this particular killer saying the victim had "ruined" something for him initially raised a warning flag for Jack. On reflection, it didn't seem so unreasonable, though. Murders were a lot less common back then, with Leclaire having been a smaller town. The entire Spokane area had grown in the intervening years. A gruesome crime like this would be especially memorable, as well as an investigation that turned out to be a genuine mystery. It had probably made a big impression on all LPD officers.

In their early thirties, Keller and Rutkowski had hardly been rookies, though. Jack turned his head to be sure no one could see his monitor, then looked to see when each had been hired. Roger Rutkowski had signed on only three years out of high school, so by the time Colleen was murdered, he'd have already had...eleven years with the Leclaire Police Department. Colleen was thirty-one at the time of her death, and Rutkowski would have been thirty-two. He hadn't been promoted to detective yet—there'd been fewer opportunities then—which meant he'd still been wearing the uniform.

Jack was a little surprised to see that the police chief had actually been hired on quite a bit later than the sergeant. He was younger, too. In fact, he was the same age as Colleen, making them classmates. They just about had to have known each other. He hadn't been at the high school her last two years, though, and he hadn't come home for more than potentially summers for a lot of years. His college degree was from Arkansas State University.

It was possible the young Dean Keller had just wanted to get away if his home life hadn't been great. He might have family in Arkansas, or had applied there to follow a girlfriend. Who knew? According to his online bio, he'd started his career in law enforcement in a small town in Tennessee, then moved on to Little Rock, Arkansas's largest city. In fact, he hadn't come home to Leclaire until a couple of years before the murder. Supposedly, Keller had returned to support a parent in ill health, which made complete sense.

So he would have been relatively new on the job when Colleen was murdered. Whatever his rank and job in Little Rock, he'd hired on here as a patrol officer, according to the records. However, he'd become a detective only a year after the murder. It was likely that he'd taken a look at the case at some point thereafter, just as the sergeant admitted he had, and Jack had in turn.

Looking seriously at these two men was probably a giant waste of time, but Jack couldn't let it go. He had to eliminate them as suspects, if only for his peace of mind.

He muffled a groan. Cops hated to admit that one of their own could have gone bad, but it happened. In this case… He tried to imagine arresting his own police chief, and covered his face with his hand.

Okay, if he were to consider either of his commanding officers as suspects, he needed to figure out what could have occurred to make them believe a well-liked woman, a "good Catholic" according to her neighbor, had ruined their lives.

At the moment, that was hard to see, as both had apparently successful careers—unless one had teetered on the brink of getting fired early on—and Rutkowski, at least, had recently passed his thirtieth wedding anniversary. Jack seemed to remember Keller had a divorce in his past. He'd check that out. If the entire marriage and divorce had taken place in Arkansas, Colleen couldn't be blamed for what had gone wrong.

Brooding, Jack made himself think logically. He should be looking at the year or two before the murder—and at the high school years, when Colleen had rather suddenly become more mature, more service oriented. Something significant had happened to change her from the typical teenager to an adult.

Yeah, he'd dig deeper…but not today. It was only three o'clock, but he'd worked many more than forty hours these past few weeks. He was going home. He had hardly slept last night. He needed to pull himself together if he was going to give his best to the investigation.

And yeah, he owed that to Gabby. He'd blown it in every other way, but she might be able to find closure—cliché though that had become—if her own effort to recover memories actually helped Jack identify and arrest the killer.

He closed his laptop, stuck it in its sleeve and under his arm, made sure his desk was otherwise bare, and started for the hall door.

Behind him, Sergeant Rutkowski called, "Cowan, hold up!"

If Rutkowski was going to give him hell for cutting out early, Jack would have a hard time swallowing it. But he turned around.

The sergeant said, "Let's go out in the hall."

It was empty at the moment.

"I had a thought," Rutkowski said. "Has Gabriella Ortiz ever tried hypnosis?"

Jack blinked. The idea had crossed his mind, but Ric had set him up to believe she was utterly resistant to remembering. He'd become fully convinced that wasn't true only yesterday, when she'd given him

such a compelling child's-eye view of the crime—
after which she kicked him out of her life.

"I haven't suggested it yet," he said.

"With a cooperative witness, someone who wants
to succeed, it can be very effective. There are issues with details recalled only under hypnosis when
it comes to trial, but we don't have to worry about
that yet." He held out a Post-it note. "Here's the name
and number for a psychologist who also does hypnosis. We've only used Dr. Adams a couple of times,
but had good luck."

Then he nodded, said, "Take Friday, too, if you
want," and went back into the squad room. With tomorrow being Thanksgiving, the sergeant must be
offering a four-day weekend. Go figure.

Jack looked down at the name. Would Gabby even
take his call?

"Uh... I talked to Jack."

Gabby was on the phone with Ric for the second
time today. The first time, this morning, she'd told
him how his good buddy, Jack Cowan, had used both
of them in pursuit of his great and noble "quest."

Ric had sounded annoyed that Jack hadn't been
straight with him, but not as outraged as she was. That
annoyed *her.* As set as her brother had always been
on her admitting what she remembered, no matter
the anguish she'd suffer, Gabby suspected he'd have
hopped readily on board Jack's plan to lie to her, if
only he'd asked nicely.

If she'd found out Ric had cooperated in the deception, too, that would have been the end of any hope of a relationship between them. She wondered if he realized that.

She, of course, had done nothing but hang around her room and stew so far today. What *could* she do? Go for a long walk to find out if someone really was willing to run her down or shoot her? An especially violent mugging would do the trick, too. Ric, of course, was at work. He'd offered to meet her for dinner, but given that they'd finally made plans to have Thanksgiving dinner at a restaurant tomorrow, she figured she could survive a day on her own.

He must be home by now. She'd just been thinking about ordering a room service meal when her phone rang for the third time this afternoon. The other two calls—and messages—were from Jack. Messages deleted unheard.

"I was just about to order dinner," she told her brother. When he expressed alarm, she said, "It occurred to me I could request a woman to bring the food to my room."

"Oh. Good thought."

Then he moved on to the purpose of his call. Unlike her, he'd been willing to talk to Jack.

"He had a suggestion I think might be a good one. Uh. I know I've been a jerk before, and if you don't want to do this, I promise I'll understand and support you. It's just…"

"Do what?"

He explained about how the police worked with a psychologist who did hypnosis, who might be able to take her back to the day of the murder. "If you can go through the same events you described to Jack but be separated from your emotional response to them—"

"Is that possible?"

"Uh… I don't actually know. I've read about how they can get you to freeze a single moment, though, so you can study what the guy is wearing, or…"

Or his face.

Reluctant as she was to admit it, this was a good idea. That's probably why Jack had been calling. She should have realized he hadn't been leaving messages because he was heartbroken and desperate for her to listen to his excuses. Nope, he still had the same goal.

Mad as she was at him, she couldn't 100 percent fault him, because she had the same goal.

"Would I have to see *him*?" she asked suspiciously.

Ric immediately knew she meant Jack. "Maybe?" Pause. "Probably. He'd almost have to be there to give the hypnotist the background and prompt her to ask particular questions."

Damn, damn, damn.

Tomorrow was Thanksgiving. Sure as shooting, no professional would go into the office until Monday, which meant Colleen would be stuck in Leclaire at least until then.

She sighed. "All right. I'll do it."

"Do you want me to call him?"

No more cowardice. "I'll do it."

"Okay." Ric sounded more cheerful. "I'll pick you up at one tomorrow."

Gabby wasn't eager to hear Jack's voice again.

Part of her knew that she'd overreacted. It had been her decision to sleep with him. He might well have seen their relationship as very casual. She hated remembering the tenderness in his voice, the times he'd comforted her, sympathized. Those made her feel most gullible.

What really hurt was that he'd let her think all those hours of talking were a mutual exploration, important to him, too. And he'd kissed her as if he meant it.

So he probably was attracted to her. She guessed he must have been, or he couldn't have... Well.

Sighing, she went to recent calls and touched his name and number. Two rings later, he answered with an urgent, "Gabby?"

"Yes. Ric passed on your suggestion that I undergo hypnosis. I wanted to let you know that I'm willing. Please schedule it as soon as you can."

"I'll do that. Gabby..."

"Let me know." With one stab, she ended the call. She'd been right—just hearing his deep voice hurt.

GABBY STARED AT the house from where she'd just parked her rental car in the driveway. She hadn't even argued when Ric called this morning and started with, "So, listen."

The gist was that after getting home from their Thanksgiving dinner and going up to his bedroom, he'd happened to glance at the square in the hall ceiling that allowed access to the partial attic. Since their father died, Ric had never had reason to go up there, or even think about it, but talking to her had awakened a memory.

"Dad made me help him put some boxes up there. He was on the ladder, and I handed them up to him."

Ric had fetched the ladder from the garage and climbed up there yesterday, finding half a dozen boxes. He'd brought them down, peeked in a few, and realized this was all Mom's stuff. "Even her clothes," he'd said, sounding squeamish.

He wanted her to go through them with him, and had carried them all downstairs this morning.

With a groan, she got out of the car, locked it and went up to the front door, which opened before she crossed the porch.

"Thanks for coming," Ric said. "Man, I'm glad I remembered about these before you left town. Just the idea of going through her clothes—" He didn't finish. Didn't have to.

Gabby felt a little bit the same, but also…excited. She'd been so young when Mom died, her memories became more insubstantial all the time. If somebody asked what her mother had been like, she couldn't have said. Maybe looking through and handling her possessions would answer some of her questions.

Following Ric inside, she saw that he'd brought the boxes into the living room, probably so that she wouldn't have to look at the kitchen. She was somewhat reassured to realize that the idea didn't horrify her the way it had. Maybe because she'd already done that, maybe because she'd brought into focus memories that had lurked in frightened corners of her mind.

Hiding hadn't helped. Facing her fears headlong had. She plopped down. "How do you want to do this?"

"Why don't you open the boxes, take things out, and once we make a decision, I'll put them in a pile depending on what it is?"

"Why do *I* get to be the leader?"

He grinned at her. "Because you're a girl? Mom was a girl?" He pushed a cardboard box closer to her.

"Oh, fine."

She unfolded the flaps and found herself looking at a jumble of items. Mostly shoes. A shoebox in pristine shape. Empty hangers, a sweater that had just been shoved in with everything else—

Gabby reached for the sweater, red, saggy and pilling. Ric's expression told her he remembered it as vividly as she did. It had been Mom's favorite to wear around the house. It really was ratty. No thrift store shopper would want it, but...

"Oh, Mom," she whispered, and hugged it to herself. Tears burned in her eyes from the powerful rush of familiarity. "I don't know what to say."

"We'll keep it." Ric's voice rasped. "Our kids can wonder why we'd keep something like this, and throw it away for us."

Gabby nodded. He took it from her and carefully folded the sweater. She thought he held it close to his face for a moment and inhaled, as if searching for a lingering perfume of their mother.

The shoes were easy, mostly too worn to interest anyone. The shoebox held a pair of black heeled sandals that didn't look as if they'd ever been worn.

They were several sizes bigger than Gabby wore, so she said, "Thrift store."

Cars passed occasionally on the street in front, but not many. A lot of neighbors were probably away for the long weekend visiting family. Gabby couldn't help thinking of Mrs. Soriano and Mr. Monroe, both of whom, in different ways, had saved her life. According to Ric, both had passed away years ago. She wished she could have seen them again, thanked them.

My fault for not coming home sooner.

They went through two boxes of Mom's clothing. Their father hadn't packed it carefully. It was as if, unable to bear looking too closely at anything, he'd grabbed everything out of the drawers and shoved it into boxes. Gabby could imagine how he'd felt. It must have been inexpressibly painful.

No garment besides the sweater rang any bells for her. She set aside a jewelry box. There was unlikely to be anything but costume jewelry in there, but she'd go through it carefully once they were otherwise done. She'd love to have a piece of jewelry to wear that reminded her of her mother.

"Did Dad bury Mom wearing her wedding and engagement rings?" she asked.

Ric moaned. "I have no idea."

The next box held books and a pair of handsome wrought iron fleur-de-lis bookends. Dad had never been much of a reader, but Gabby vaguely recalled her mother was. Mom was mostly the one to read to her kids, too.

Picking up the book on the top, Gabby said, "Poetry. I had no idea—"

She turned her head sharply and listened. She didn't hear anything, but...a shadow had passed in front of the window.

Ric was staring in the same direction. "Gabby," he said quietly, "I think there's someone on the porch. Grab your phone and run for the back of the house. Now."

She responded to the intensity in that last word and reached down for her phone poking out of the front pocket of her handbag. Then she jumped onto the sofa to bypass the boxes and tore for the kitchen.

Behind her, glass shattered and she heard a muffled *pop, pop, pop*, followed by a thud.

From the refuge of the kitchen, she screamed, "Ric!"

No answer.

Chapter Fourteen

Normally, Jack would have had Thanksgiving with his father. He really hadn't been in the mood, though, either for the drive or for celebrating anything. Part of that was his pain at losing any chance with Gabby, but more important was a raging frustration that she was on her own with a killer hunting her.

He kept reasoning with himself. The near hit-and-run really might have been a close call because of a distracted driver. Any cop knew how often that kind of carelessness resulted in tragedy. The man who'd tried to persuade her to let him into her hotel room was another story, though.

Yesterday, he'd known she was spending part of the day with Ric. That wasn't perfect; Ric didn't carry a gun and had no bodyguard or combat training. Still. Gabby should be safe in her hotel room, if she just stayed put.

Yeah, but she had to eat.

Thanksgiving had sucked, as far as he was concerned. If he hadn't gone about this all wrong, he could have invited Ric and Gabby to his place for their Thanksgiving meal. Never having cooked a turkey before, he might have had to take a speed lesson, or begged her or Ric for help, but they'd have had fun.

Instead, he'd microwaved a couple of burritos.

Today, his skin crawled with anxiety. Surely she was being careful—but what was she doing? If only the psychologist had been able to see Gabby today, but no, she and her husband had flown to Phoenix to celebrate with his parents. Monday morning was the soonest she could get Gabby in, and she was shuffling appointments to manage that.

By now, Jack couldn't settle down to anything. He should have gone into the station. He did finally receive a call letting him know that the security officer who'd been arrested but not charged with rape had lived in the Houston area for the last fifteen years, and was wheelchair bound after a stroke he'd had the previous year.

One more name Jack could cross off his list.

He started for the kitchen to pour himself a cup of coffee, but found himself pacing instead.

Would Gabby answer if he called? What about Ric?

He reached the front door and turned back just as his phone, left on the kitchen table, rang. It could be anyone, but— He moved fast, pouncing on it when he saw Gabby's name. What did a call from her mean?

"Gabby?"

"Ric's been shot." Her breath hitched with what he guessed was a sob. "I'm at his house. We were

going through some more of Mom's things, and—
Can you come?"

"You called 9-1-1?"

"Yes. I was lucky because a patrol officer was really close, but the ambulance isn't here yet, and I'm scared. I...don't know how badly Ric is injured."

"I'm on my way." Jack snatched up his wallet and keys and went out the door. "Stay on the line with me if you don't need to make any other calls. I should be there in ten to fifteen minutes." Or less, if he stepped on it.

"I'll be a distraction." Already she'd collected herself, or else he was hearing a chill in her voice. "I'm okay. Drive safe." Call ended.

He swore pungently as he leaped into his SUV and backed out of the garage.

GABBY DROPPED THE phone on the coffee table and went back to Ric's side. He was breathing. Thank God he was alive, but the police officer was applying pressure to a bloody mess on his shoulder and chest. It looked as if he'd hit his head on a corner of the hearth as he went down. She could see a smear of blood on the brick.

Realizing she was rocking, she made herself stop. "What's taking so long?"

The extremely young officer's expression betrayed more stress than he'd like to know. "I think I hear a siren."

"I do, too." She squeezed Ric's slack hand. "Hold on, Ric. I'm here."

Through the broken front window, she saw an ambulance rocket to a stop, then back into the driveway beside her rental. Thank God she'd left room. Barely a minute later, a man and woman appeared on the porch.

Their dark blue uniforms disturbed her on a fundamental level, just as the young officer's had. She had to shake off her reaction. Seconds later, she scooted away on her butt to give them room to evaluate Ric. They asked a couple of quick questions, applied fresh dressings, and with barely disguised urgency prepared him for transport.

Her gaze glued to her wounded brother, Gabby heard a squeal of brakes but didn't look up until Jack appeared in the open doorway. He looked straight at her, but spoke briefly with the EMTs before stepping aside so they could wheel Ric out.

Then Jack came to her, crouching so that he didn't tower over her. "I think he'll be fine."

"I have to go to the hospital!" she said frantically, jumping to her feet.

Jack gripped her arms. "Nobody there will be able to talk to you for a little while. Ric will be rushed into surgery. You won't do him any good sitting in a waiting room. Take a minute, calm down and tell me what happened."

Her first impulse was to fight off his hands, but she closed her eyes, focused on the strength in those hands, the steadiness in his voice, and nodded. When he nudged her to sit at the opposite end of the sofa from where she'd been before, she plopped down, watching him take a seat on the coffee table in front of her.

"Won't there be crime scene investigators?" she asked. "Should we be here?"

"This is my scene, and this should be fine for a few minutes. I'm not about to drag you into the kitchen."

She bobbed her head, held on tightly to her phone and waited.

It didn't take long to answer his questions. He could see the pile of boxes, opened and unopened. The glistening blood pooled where Ric had sprawled on the oak floor.

At least it would wipe up easily, she thought, in that annoying way the mind worked at times like this. If Ric didn't survive, cleaning up the mess would become meaningless.

Jack's question reined in her thoughts. "Are these boxes from the storage unit?"

She shook her head and told him about Ric remembering that some boxes had been stowed up in the attic space. "Once he realized they all held Mom's possessions, he asked if I'd help go through them."

Jack shifted gears. "When he told you to run, did Ric intend to follow you?"

"I assumed so," she said uncertainly.

"That's likely, but you had quite a head start."

She told him how she'd used the sofa to leap over the top of the boxes. Sitting there, she saw that one box had been knocked askew. "He must have stumbled over it."

Jack wanted her to show him how far she'd gotten.

When she led him toward the hall, where the staircase rose and doorways opened to the kitchen and the utility room as well as the back door, he stopped and swore.

"That one must have barely missed you."

"What?" Her gaze followed his to the bullet hole in the wallboard. Her eyes were level with it. Feeling sick, she said, "I didn't know."

"Okay, sweetheart, that's it. I'll take you to the hospital."

"I can drive."

He studied her, those blue eyes penetrating. "Do you feel steady enough?"

She took a deep breath, analyzed how she felt and nodded. "The angrier I get, the better I feel."

His smile was both gentle and approving. It might have made her knees a little wobbly, if they hadn't already been. She stiffened them and followed him out the front door.

She started to go back for her handbag, but Jack did it for her. He stopped to talk for a few minutes to the responding officer, who nodded several times.

Then she started her car, backed out into the street and fell in behind his Tahoe as he led the way to the hospital. She'd noticed signs pointing to it, but hadn't been sure where it was.

Once there, it turned out he'd been right that Ric had been whisked immediately into surgery. Jack requested, and got, a private waiting room for her that was behind the swinging doors into the surgery unit.

He nodded his thanks to the nurse who'd brought them there. "This should be safe."

Sitting on one of four upholstered chairs surrounding a table, she said, "Safe?"

He took the chair right next to hers. "I don't want you sitting out there in plain sight."

"Oh." She pictured herself as a bottle set up on a fence rail for target practice. They could have been followed, or the killer might have logically assumed this was where she'd be. He must have seen Ric go down. "Hadn't you better go back?"

As Jack regarded her, Gabby noticed for the first time how strained he looked. He might have aged a decade, furrows appearing.

"Yeah. I do have to. Gabby...don't go anywhere, with anyone."

"I'm not that dumb."

"I know you aren't." He ran a hand over his face, but didn't look any better when he was done. "You scared the shit out of me. Again."

Old anger bubbled up. "Afraid you'd lose your witness?"

"You know better than that. I meant every word I said to you. Think about that." Shaking his head, he rose to his feet. "I'll be back later. Wait here for me."

The door opened, closed and he was gone.

Leaving her filled with dread, her thoughts spiraling between the brother with whom she'd just reconnected and Jack. A man whose devastation she couldn't deny.

LOADING THE BOXES into his SUV a couple of hours later, Jack reverted to brooding about Gabby. Yeah, he'd screwed up, but did she really believe he was cold-blooded enough to care only that she was a critical witness in a murder investigation? Hadn't she noticed that he'd crossed town in half the time it should have taken, desperate to see with his own eyes that she was okay?

His phone rang. Gabby, at last. Ric had still been in surgery an hour ago when Jack had last called her.

"He's in recovery," she said, before he could get in a *hello*. "Ric's chances are good, but there was a lot of damage. He was hit by two bullets. The surgeon kept thinking he could close, and they'd realize there was still bleeding somewhere." Words kept tumbling out. "The head injury might be the greatest threat. He hit that hearth hard enough to fracture his skull."

"He's tough, Gabby. In great physical condition, which will help in his recovery."

"There's some swelling around his brain." Now she sounded almost numb. "They might have to punch a hole in his skull to…to let fluid drain."

Crap. "I know you're scared. Have faith, sweetheart."

She gave a broken laugh. "Is this when I start praying?"

"Haven't you already?"

Silence, which was its own answer.

"I'll be there in just a few minutes." He shut the hatch door. "I arranged for someone to nail plywood over the window."

"Front and back now."

"Yeah." He almost said, *Somebody has it in for you big-time*, but knew she already had to be thinking the same—unless she was stuck on the fact that her brother had taken two bullets meant for her.

"I'll see you when you get here."

Making phone calls the whole way, Jack obeyed speed limits this time. He parked right in front of the emergency room entrance at the hospital in a slot saved for law enforcement. He doubted the killer had hung around to see him load the boxes, but Jack still wanted his Tahoe highly visible from the ER.

Upstairs, he suffered a jolt when he found the private waiting room empty, but when he snagged the first passing nurse, she told him Gabby had been allowed into recovery to see Ric.

Ten minutes later, Gabby reappeared. The sight of her hit him hard. Her skin looked as if it had been stretched tight over her facial bones and her eyes were sunken, accented by dark half circles beneath them. Hair stuck out here and there from her usually smooth braid. Her lips lacked color.

Wordless, he held out his arms. His heart cramped painfully when she hesitated, but at last she walked right to him. As he pulled her close, she wrapped both her arms around him and laid her head on his chest.

Jack didn't ask any questions, just offered physical comfort. Embracing her gave him comfort, too. Maybe she'd forgive him. The feel of her curves, the citrus scent of the glossy, if disheveled, hair beneath his cheek, her trust, they all gave him hope.

Finally she sighed, and he had to relax his arms enough to let her step back. She looked up at him with shadowed eyes, and said, "He's still unconscious."

"He did just have surgery," he reminded her.

"Yes, but…he should have opened his eyes by now."

"It's not a surprise that he hasn't."

"That's what the surgeon said, but… I let myself think…"

"Hey." He tugged her over to the chairs, sat them down and shifted his chair so he faced her and could hold both her hands. "You have to give him time. Aren't the doctors you've talked to optimistic?"

"Yes, but I'm afraid they're lying to me." A couple of tears trembled on her lashes, and she swiped them away impatiently. "Did you find anything?"

"Nothing useful." The frustration he'd pushed down gained power again, like a flash flood. "We've got a couple of bullets, of course, but they're a common caliber. The surgeon saved the two he dug out of Ric, although they're not in great shape. The bullets are only useful when we have a gun to match them to. Otherwise…" Jack shook his head. "He fired through the glass from the front porch. Probably didn't touch anything. With him using a suppressor, the few neighbors who were home didn't hear a damn thing, except for a woman halfway down the block who went to her front window because she heard the roar of an engine accelerating to what had to be dangerous speed. They've had trouble with teenagers speeding, she says. She did get a glimpse of the vehicle, but of course not of the license plate."

"Let me guess. It was a giant black SUV?"

He grimaced. "She told me it looked kind of like mine."

"If only there'd been a traffic camera there or where he tried to run me down."

If only were two of the saddest words in the English language.

"I'd like you to come home with me," Jack said.

Gabby reared back. "Now?"

"No, I don't expect you to leave right this minute, but I don't want you at the hotel anymore. It's not safe for you to come and go."

She blinked. "Then...what?"

"My house."

Jack didn't much like the way she scrutinized him, but he withstood her inspection.

"I don't suppose I have a lot of choices, do I?"

"No."

After a moment, she nodded. "I don't suppose you're going to give me directions to your house and head home."

"No, but if you'll give me your room key, I'll go get your stuff from the hotel and check you out. I don't want you going near that place."

Her teeth closed on her lower lip, but she nodded. It took him a minute to realize she was trying to tug her hands free. When he let go, she dug in her bag and handed him the room card. "I'm in 328."

"I remember. I'll see you in about half an hour."

He hoped like hell her brother hurried to regain consciousness.

STILL SCARED, GABBY had finally agreed to go home with Jack. With Ric in Intensive Care, she was allowed to sit with him for only a few minutes an hour. Around ten o'clock, Jack put his foot down. Today had been enormously stressful. She was so tired, she wasn't steady on her feet, he declared.

Unfortunately, he was right. That didn't keep her from feeling she was abandoning Ric, but in all honesty, with him still unconscious, her presence wasn't doing him a speck of good. She wished he had a girlfriend who'd want to take shifts at the hospital, or that she knew who any of his best friends were.

This time, Jack wouldn't let her drive, although he promised to bring her back in the morning. Something in his expression made her wonder if she would see her rental car any time in the immediate future. He didn't have to hint again that she might as well paint a target on herself if she walked out of the hospital and cut through the parking lot to the car. The shooting had been on the local news, with a promised update at ten o'clock. If the killer had thought for a minute she was down, too, he knew better now. He also knew where he could find her for the immediate future: the hospital.

Maybe she should call the rental company and ask them to pick up the car.

Gabby was weary enough not to object when Jack put his hands around her waist and lifted her up onto the seat before closing the door and going around to the driver side. However briefly the overhead light had been on, she'd seen enough to have her twisting to look back at the cargo space. There was her suit-case, tote and laptop case, but also…

Jack saw what she was looking at. "Put on your seat belt. Yes, that's the stuff you and Ric were going through. I'm taking it home so you and I can finish finding out what's in those boxes."

Gabby pulled the seat belt over herself before saying, "You think there might be something in there that's important."

He backed out, then shot her a glance she could see because the area right in front of the ER was brightly lit. "I do think that."

Her mind might be moving slowly, but it trudged determinedly on. "That's why you went to the stor-age unit with us."

"Partly. I also wanted to be sure no one could get to you."

No wonder he'd parked the way he had, and paced out in the cold instead of joining them inside the unit.

"Did you go through the stuff you were supposed to take to the dump?"

"Some of it," he admitted. "I didn't unwrap the plastic around the artificial Christmas tree."

Despite the sheer awfulness of this day, the wry humor in his voice almost made her laugh. If only she didn't like Jack so much.

If only… But she didn't let herself complete that wish.

Chapter Fifteen

Saturday afternoon, Ric groaned, rolled his head on the thin pillow, and opened his eyes.

Gabby leaped to her feet from the hard plastic chair next to the hospital bed. "Ric!"

He squinted at her. Worked his mouth a few times, then said, "Gab?"

Had his mind shorted out halfway through her name, or did he remember the whole family calling her that because of her nonstop chatter?

On the verge of tears, she smiled. "I've been scared for you."

"Why—?" He took in the room. "Hospital?"

"Yes."

She saw the instant it came back to him.

"Shot."

"Yes." Gabby sniffed. "Because you got in the way of bullets intended for me."

"That's...what...brothers...are...for."

"Who knew?" she said, almost lightly. "Your mouth is dry, isn't it? I'd better let the nurse know you're back with us. And Jack. He's out in the waiting room. He hopes you saw something I didn't."

"Wish."

She rushed out of the cubicle, which promptly filled with medical personnel. As soon as she emerged through the double doors, Jack closed his laptop and stood.

"He's awake?"

"How did you know?"

He grinned. "You're glowing."

"It's such a relief." It had become habit to walk into his arms and draw strength from him. "The doctor is with him right now."

"Is he coherent?"

"Yes." She gave a teary smile. "He called me *Gab*."

His chest vibrated with a laugh beneath her cheek. "I'd forgotten that. We'd be pulling up to the house, and there you'd be waiting. He'd mumble, 'Gab, Gab, Gab.'"

"I haven't heard that in so long."

"I'll give them a few minutes, then ask to talk to him."

At the returning somberness, she straightened. "I don't think he saw anything."

When she explained, Jack grimaced. "The guy was bound to have his face covered anyway."

Nearly fifteen minutes passed before a nurse came out to say that Detective Cowan could speak to Ric. Jack insisted on bringing Gabby, of course. He hadn't left her alone in any public areas of the hospital all day, even though he must have better things to do than sit there.

He and Ric clasped hands and held on. It turned out that Ric had seen more than she had, but only a large, black-clad figure and what he was sure was a gun.

"Weird long barrel."

"Suppressor."

Ric nodded and winced.

Jack updated him with what little they'd learned and told him that he and Gabby would go through the boxes in case their mother had left any clue to the reason for her murder.

Ric looked at her. "Bet you've been here all day."

"Of course I have!"

"You look like crap. Take a nap. My head is pounding. I'm going to take some of the good stuff—" he lifted the button that would send pain relief flooding through his body "—and sleep myself. Doctor said they wouldn't transfer me to a regular room until morning."

"Fine. I don't need to watch you sleep." Gabby leaned over and kissed her brother's stubbly cheek. "Thank you," she whispered.

He lifted the hand with the IV needle to her jaw. "Sister."

Jack steered her out, told the nurse they were leaving and made sure she had both their phone numbers, and escorted Gabby through the maze of corridors to the ER entrance. There, he stepped outside alone and studied the surroundings before waving her out to his SUV.

Once they were driving, he said, "Part of me wants to start work on those boxes, but Ric's right. You need a nap and a decent dinner."

"I can hold out."

He shook his head. "Not necessary. This evening or the morning will be soon enough."

Gabby didn't argue. Last night, after barely managing to brush her teeth, she'd gone to bed in Jack's guest room and plunged into a state more akin to unconsciousness than sleep. Unfortunately, she'd woken up four hours later and only drifted in and out of restless sleep the remainder of the night. Ric was right; when she'd looked in the mirror this morning, she'd made a face at herself. She did not look good.

When they neared his house, Jack had her unfasten her seat belt and crouch down on the floorboards, just as he had last evening and again when they left for the hospital this morning. Not until they were in the garage and the door had descended did he tell her she could get up. She had yet to see the outside of his house, although she knew from the interior that it probably dated to the same era as the neighborhood where she'd grown up. This morning when she came downstairs, she'd discovered blinds were drawn so no one could see in—and she couldn't look out at the porch or yard, either.

The house couldn't be more than half-furnished, but had beautifully refinished hardwood floors, fireplace mantel, moldings and some built-in bookcases and, in the dining room, an original built-in buffet. She couldn't understand why he hadn't done more to make it feel like home.

Now, though, she only trudged upstairs, visited the guest bathroom and flopped down on the bed.

Laying her head on the pillow felt blissful. She pulled the quilt over herself and let the weariness wash over her, along with the memories of the day. Ric smiled. He kissed her cheek. He was going to be fine. She was smiling when she fell over the edge.

JACK FELT A little ragged, too, but he could sleep tonight. He frequently missed a night's sleep in the urgent hours after a murder.

When the quiet upstairs told him Gabby had gone to sleep, he went back to his research. He hadn't lost his uneasiness where Sergeant Rutkowski and Chief Keller were concerned, but he'd backed off somewhat on his suspicion. Rutkowski's suggestion that Gabby try hypnosis wasn't something the killer would do.

Except, Jack reminded himself, that two days later, there was an open attempt on her life. Rutkowski had to have known the psychologist wouldn't be able to get Gabby in over a holiday weekend, giving him time to go on the attack.

Would he have told Chief Keller what he'd suggested? Jack couldn't think of a good way to ask, and wouldn't have the chance until at least Monday anyway.

Right now, Jack was intent on finding out what he could about a series of rapes that had occurred in the region back when Colleen had been in high school. Those rapes had been spread over five police jurisdictions and, as was too often the case, those agencies hadn't communicated with each other. Not until near the end had anyone connected the crimes. None of those rapes had happened in Leclaire, four had been in the greater Spokane area, and one across the border in Idaho. Descriptions and MO suggested one man had committed all the crimes.

All had been young girls, the youngest fifteen, the oldest twenty. Because so many women didn't report rapes even now, Jack suspected the guy had raped more women. Unfortunately, none of the reported crimes had been date rapes, when the victim could have named her assailant. Instead, women alone at night had been grabbed from behind and dragged either into the bushes or the back of a van. The rapist had worn a face mask. All the victims said he was big. "Huge," the fifteen-year-old had declared.

Crime victims invariably described their assailants as larger than they actually were, so Jack took that with a grain of salt. Still, the description did jibe with his observation of the hotel security camera footage. There was no question the man who'd tried to get into Gabby's room had been big—as tall as Jack's six-foot-two, and possibly broader.

Jack hunted down every scrap of information he could find on the long-ago rapes. What if this creep had also committed date rape, but intimidated or blackmailed his victims into keeping their mouths closed?

About the time Colleen had become quieter and more mature, the rapes had either stopped or no more young women found the courage to report them. Plenty of rapes had still been investigated, of course, but none sounded as if they'd been committed by the same man.

His mind took a logical, if disquieting, jump to the man who had left Leclaire not long after the last rape. Would it turn out there'd been similar rapes in Little Rock, Arkansas, during the years when Dean Keller had lived there? Trouble was, the only way he'd get the kind of details he needed was to call a detective there and ask him to delve into records. Explaining why he wanted them, though, that got touchy. They'd want a reason—and a name—before they committed to that kind of time. It wasn't hard to imagine the request getting back to Keller.

Goodbye, job.

Deciding to think about it, Jack started dinner. He enjoyed cooking when he had the time, which was rare. Once the spicy vegetarian chili simmering on the stove started to smell good, he stuck corn bread in the oven.

When Gabby appeared in the living room, he saw with approval that some of the strain had left her face and she'd obviously brushed her hair and braided it anew. The exhaustion and fear for her brother that she couldn't hide had had the benefit of helping Jack rein in his physical response to her the last two days, but now he felt the familiar punch. He loved every one of her curves, that glorious hair, her pretty mouth and the sparkle of gold in otherwise green eyes. Yeah, and now he knew what she looked like naked. How she'd responded to his touch.

If his voice was a little rough, he couldn't help it. "You got some sleep?"

"Yes, thank you. Something smells good."

"Should be ready." In fact, by the time he'd set the table, the oven timer had gone off, and they sat down in the kitchen to eat.

Gabby was very willing to continue going through the boxes, although she did say, "I wish Ric was here, in case I come across something meaningful to him."

"We won't throw anything away immediately. Once he's out of the hospital, he can take a look himself."

Later, when they'd finished dinner, Gabby sank down at one end of the sofa. He brought the first box to her, then joined her on the sofa close enough to look over her shoulder.

"More clothes," she said in disappointment. She was careful to lift every garment out of the box, however, and neatly fold it, restoring the piles to the box when she was done.

The next carton held pieces of her and Ric's childhoods: ratty stuffed animals, artwork sent home from elementary school, homemade Mother's Day cards and report cards. Gabby laughed a few times, got teary, and finally closed it all back up. "I'll want to keep some of this, and I'm sure Ric will, too."

She decided to go through the boxes of books later and decide what to keep. She admired two different sets of bookends, but put them back in the boxes for now. "I'll keep those unless Ric wants them."

Jack had brought the jewelry chest Gabby had left sitting on the coffee table at Ric's house. She did flip through the contents now, in case her mother had an unknown stash of valuable jewels. The only item of interest was a sterling silver charm bracelet that held only two charms, a tiny football and a book that hung open but looked like it might close.

"Isn't that strange?" Gabby murmured. "It's so tarnished. Well, I guess it would be after twenty-five years."

Or forty years, Jack speculated. "Do you recognize it?" he asked.

Gabby shook her head. "I doubt she'd have worn it, since it was only a…a starter bracelet. I mean, if Dad gave it to her, he'd have kept giving her charms, wouldn't he?"

"Yeah. And the book charm was obviously meant for her—you said she liked to read—but your dad never played football, did he?"

He bet Roger Rutkowski and Dean Keller had.

Gabby shook her head. "Heavens, no! Dad was only five-foot-six, you know. Mom never wore heels, because she was already a bit taller than him."

Jack had prepared himself with evidence bags, and he had Gabby drop the bracelet into a small one. The tiny book was the only part with a smooth enough surface to conceivably hold even a partial fingerprint, but that could be enough to be helpful.

Gabby looked askance, but didn't ask why he wanted to keep it.

The very last box held the treasure trove Jack had hoped for. Photo albums, a couple of high school yearbooks, two chocolate boxes repurposed to hold letters, notes and some loose photos. While Gabby started scanning the letters, Jack took Colleen's freshman yearbook and flipped to a photo of the football team. Sure enough, there was a very young Rutkowski and—it took him a moment to recognize the other face—Dean Keller, too. Dean had been a freshman, big enough to play varsity instead of JV, Rutkowski a sophomore. Jack found Colleen's freshman photo and recognized her smile as one that hid braces. He'd worn them himself, and hated every minute of it.

Then he studied the two boys' photos. Rutkowski had been homely even as a boy. Dean Keller had apparently always been handsome with an air of assurance not many kids that age possessed. As good-looking as he was, would he have bothered with a freshman girl with a mouthful of metal? Jack doubted it.

A year later, though… He reached for the next yearbook, then realized it was from Colleen's senior year. Maybe the other two were at the bottom of the box.

"This is weird," Gabby announced.

"What?"

She handed him a letter still in an envelope. The return address was the rectory at St. Stephen's Catholic Church. Jack unfolded the letter and attempted to decipher the spidery handwriting. It was addressed to "Dear Colleen" and signed "Father Ambrose."

It wasn't only the handwriting that had Jack struggling to understand the body of the letter. Father Ambrose wrote in a way Colleen presumably would have understood, but wouldn't give away any secrets if one of her parents had read the letter.

He regretted that he'd had no chance to speak to Colleen privately. As she might know, he had been transferred and would be moving away. He hoped for assurance that she was doing well, and that the measures he'd taken had sufficed to allow her to live with confidence and peace of heart. He encouraged her to call if there was anything at all he could do for her, but he had complete faith in his successor, Father Paul, whom she had already met. He closed by saying, "Go with God, child."

Jack reread the letter. What "measures" had a Catholic priest taken to protect a teenage girl in his parish?

Gabby made an awful sound. Jack turned his head to see shock on her face. She thrust a manila envelope at him, the flap open.

Jack dropped the letter and took the envelope. There was no mistaking a pair of flower-print bikini panties of another era. This time, he took a moment to don a plastic glove before he gingerly lifted out the panties. The fabric in the crotch was starting to break down from whatever had stained it in addition to a nickel-sized rusty splotch that had to be old blood. Jack would have bet anything Colleen had gotten home, rushed to her room and torn these off. She might have shoved them out of sight for a while, or had had the presence of mind to decide immediately to preserve them. Even in shock and sickened, she'd have known about DNA tracing. This had to be semen, and the blood from her having lost her virginity.

What his father had overheard came to Jack, word for word.

If you keep bothering me, you should know I kept evidence. I won't hesitate to take it to the police.

The panties on their own wouldn't be conclusive; the sex act could have been consensual. But if she'd told anyone that she'd been raped... Oh, yeah, that could definitely ruin a guy's life.

His gaze turned back to the letter that lay on his lap. For whatever reason, she had told someone: her priest.

And he'd taken measures.

GABBY HAD HERSELF tied in knots by Monday morning. The idea of letting herself be hypnotized freaked her out. To lose control of her own mind...why had she agreed to this?

And then there were the appalling discoveries she had made in a box of her mother's mementos. If only Dad had looked through them instead of just packing up everything, he might have been able to help the police find Mom's murderer. It would have been a lot easier to track down Father Ambrose twenty-five years ago.

Dad couldn't possibly have known she'd been raped as a teenager, or he'd have told one of the detectives. Why, why, had Mom pretended it never happened? Kept proof that it had, but not reported the crime? Did she blame herself, as so many women did? Believed she'd given implicit permission just because she'd sneaked out to meet up with her rapist? Worn clothing her mother had called suggestive?

If she really had sneaked out, versus gone on an approved date, the lie to her parents might explain why she didn't dare tell them. Since Gabby hadn't known her grandparents, she had no way of knowing how strict they'd been, how they'd have reacted to their daughter's rape.

Gabby felt sick just thinking what her mother had gone through.

Ric, at least, was doing well. Gabby and Jack had spent several hours with him at the hospital yesterday. Well, really, she'd spent time with her brother while Jack had sat in a corner hunched over his laptop, fingers flying. Occasionally he'd made phone calls, speaking just quietly enough she couldn't hear what he was saying.

But she knew he was trying to track down Father Ambrose, the priest who'd been transferred to another parish something like forty years ago. From what Jack said, Father Ambrose would probably be in his late sixties or older by now. Would he be retired, or did priests typically continue holding worship and counseling their parishioners until they were physically unable?

Now, Jack said, "We're here." He turned into the parking lot beside a medical building.

She wanted to say, *I can't do this*, but knew she wouldn't. Besides visiting Ric, yesterday Gabby had spent hours poring over her mother's photo albums, yearbooks, letters from friends and even the diary she'd kept in middle school and into her freshman year in high school. Gabby had believed she'd lost all chance to really know her mother, but she'd been wrong. And by God, she'd do anything in the world now to see the man who'd raped her mother and then, years later, murdered her arrested and imprisoned. That fury would see her through with this.

Jack held her hand as they walked into the building and took the elevator to the second floor. Before the doors slid open, he looked at her. "Are you okay with this?"

Gabby gave a sharp nod, and he kissed her, briefly, gently, and then he walked her into the psychologist's office.

DR. JOSEPHINE ADAMS spoke first to Jack while Gabby waited in another room. He told the woman everything he knew Gabby had seen, and suggested details that might well be buried in her mind. Then she allowed him to join her once she had successfully hypnotized Gabby, but cautioned him to stay out of sight and not say a word unless it was absolutely essential.

Gabby lay comfortably on an upholstered chaise lounge. He'd seen fleeting instances before of her regressing to the child who'd been watching her mother be butchered, but she had immediately swung back to being the adult Gabby. The woman he loved. This time, even her expressions were childlike, her voice slightly too high.

The pivotal moment came when the killer had passed closest to where Gabby had been hiding in the utility room. In the telling Gabby rushed past it, just as she had when she'd told Jack what she'd seen. But this time, Dr. Adams said calmly, "You know how to pause a video tape, don't you, Gabby?"

"Uh-huh."

"Stop what you're seeing right here."

Gabby nodded obediently.

"Now let's rewind, just a little bit, until you first see him walking into sight. He's dressed in dark blue, carrying a garbage bag. What color is the bag?"

"It's black."

"And is it full?"

Gabby's forehead crinkled. "Not really *full*, but there's stuff in it."

"All right. He takes a step or two and turns his head to look your way. Let's pause there again."

"He sees me," she said in panic. "He has to see me. He's looking right at me!"

"He's looking at the pile of dirty clothes," Dr. Adams said calmly. "He doesn't know you're hiding there."

Gabby took a deep breath.

"You said he's wearing a hat."

"Uh-huh."

"What does the hat look like?"

"It's blue. The part that sticks out over his face is shiny."

Jack's jaw was so tight, he expected a molar to crack. Damn, damn.

"Who wears hats like that, Gabby?"

"Daddy was in the navy." Her tone suggested she wasn't quite sure what that was. "There's a picture on the mantel of him in his uniform. He wore a hat like that, 'cept it was white."

"Anyone else you can think of?"

"A police officer who came to talk to Ric's class did. Mommy and I took treats that day and got to hear him."

"Very good," Dr. Adams said warmly. "While the man is frozen in front of you, can you see his face?"

"Only the bottom part. A little bit of his nose and…" She lifted a hand to indicate her jaw.

"Even after men shave, you can usually see what color the stubble is."

"Uh-huh. Daddy's is practically *black*."

"What about this man?"

"It's hard to see. He must've shaved this morning." She frowned. "It's brown, not gold like Sarah's daddy's."

Jack let out a long breath. Dr. Adams gave him a warning look. She asked a few more questions, about the day the car jumped up on the sidewalk and almost ran Gabby down, but then she cycled back instead to the blood spraying each time the man thrust his hand down. After a minute, the psychologist said,

"All right, Gabby. I'm going to count down, and you'll wake up. Five, four, three, two, one."

Gabby blinked a few times, and her expression changed, becoming wholly adult. "Are we done?"

Dr. Adams smiled. "We're done. You did splendidly, Gabby."

Gabby sat up and swung her feet to the floor. That's when she saw Jack. She'd never looked more vulnerable than she did when she said, "Can we go home?"

To his house. He had to clear his throat before he could say, "You bet."

He thanked the doctor, and he and Gabby held hands all the way out to the car, neither saying a word.

Chapter Sixteen

Jack's tension had to be infecting her. From the minute he left her at his house, she jumped at every sound from the street and inside the house. The furnace startled her every time it came on, which was frequent given the cold weather. Having the windows covered so that nobody could see inside should have been comforting, but if anything, it had the reverse effect. She desperately wanted to peek between the blinds or around the edge of a curtain, but what if *he* was outside and saw? The words *dead giveaway* popped into her mind, making her shiver.

Not a soul knew she was staying at Jack's house, which made the likelihood of an attack here next to nonexistent, but logic didn't help.

At least Jack had left her with something useful to do this afternoon.

After the hypnosis session, the two of them had stopped to see Ric at the hospital, then ate lunch at a Greek restaurant Jack liked. She could tell he hated to leave her alone, but he'd decided he really needed to go into the station.

"I haven't even begun the paperwork on the shooting at your brother's house," Jack grumbled. "And you never know, our crime scene people might have magically found something."

Gabby shooed him out the door. If she hadn't, well, she was deeply afraid they'd have ended up in bed together. It was still possible they would tonight, but at least she'd have a little while to weigh the pros and cons. Number one on the "con" list being the anger and sense of betrayal that still simmered somewhere deep inside.

She wrinkled her nose. She was afraid not even the anger would help once Jack kissed her. Because on the "plus" side, he had come running when she called, bared his deep fear for her and given her everything she needed since.

Walling off her tangle of emotions, she made herself focus. The task he'd left with her was to continue the hunt for the priest.

Jack had found Father Ambrose's second posting, at St. Florian's in Detroit, but after ten years he'd been moved again. Nobody currently there had known him. Given that yesterday was Sunday, he hadn't been in contact with the archdiocese till this morning. That person had trouble accessing the records, but determined Father Ambrose had gone to a church in Haverhill, Massachusetts.

Taking up where he'd left off, she worked her laptop and phone, making call after call. Father Ambrose, Gabby finally learned, had retired just a year ago from his fifth church, this one in Boston. The man who gave her the information believed Father Ambrose had inherited a house somewhere in New England from his parents, but he would have to do further research to get contact information. Gabby wondered if he had to obtain permission from above before handing out contact info. That would make sense. She didn't believe for a minute that the archdiocese would lose track of their priests the minute they retired.

She mulled over possibilities. The priest presumably hadn't been named Ambrose at birth. Would he have returned to his birth name, or held on to Ambrose? She couldn't quite imagine him having a Facebook page, and doubted priests used LinkedIn to communicate with their fellow priests. Still, she did a search for an Ambrose Kearney in Massachusetts, then some neighboring states.

Nada.

She pulled up white pages, got nowhere. Maybe Jack would have better resources.

Astonishingly, at four thirty her time, her phone rang. Father Ambrose now lived in Pawtucket, Rhode Island, and still filled in for services in the St. Mary's Parish. Gabby had an address and phone number.

When Jack came in the door after six o'clock, looking tired, she said triumphantly, "I have a phone number."

Some of the weariness on his face eased. "Seriously? Did you talk to him?"

He followed her to the kitchen, where she put the leftover chili on the stove to heat and popped the corn bread in the microwave while explaining that she'd left a message with Father Ambrose. Jack disappeared to change from slacks, dress shirt and tie to jeans and a faded Seattle Seahawks sweatshirt.

When they sat down to eat, she asked about his afternoon, and got a grimace. "Pretty worthless."

She buttered her corn bread. "What if he doesn't remember Mom? It's been an awful lot of years."

"I'd like to say that's the kind of thing that sticks in your memory, but priests must constantly deal with troubled teenagers, the aftereffects of suicide, dysfunctional families…" He sighed. "We can only hope. Did you leave my name and number as well as yours?"

Gabby nodded.

Conversation lagged as they'd finished eating.

Jack's phone rang. "My father," he said briefly. "Leave the cleanup to me…"

"Don't be silly. It won't take five minutes."

"Thanks." He stood, kissed her cheek and answered the phone. "Dad?"

Although he wandered into the living room, she could still hear his side of the conversation.

"Gabby's father had boxed up all of Colleen's stuff and stuck it up in the attic," he said. "We found enough to believe she was raped in high school. I think it has to be connected. She knew and dreaded seeing the man who killed her."

Gabby missed some of what Jack said when she ran hot water to wash the pan and rinse off their bowls and plates before putting them in the dishwasher.

"There's no question she's being targeted." He sounded grim now. "Friday, this guy walked onto the porch at the house where Ric Ortiz still lives and shot through the front window. Missed Gabby by inches but badly injured her brother. He's going to be okay but had emergency surgery and was just moved out of the ICU yesterday."

A couple of grunts followed. Then, "What am I doing to protect her? What do you think? She's staying here with me, of course." After a moment, "No, of course that's not usual practice—"

Done in the kitchen, Gabby hovered just outside the living room, not wanting to interrupt but assuming he didn't care that she could hear what he was saying, or he'd have gone to his bedroom. Even though he had his back to her, Jack turned as if he sensed her presence. The way those blue eyes locked on to her got to her as much as it had in the restaurant that first night.

"You're right," he said into the phone. "It is sort of ironic, isn't it?" He listened to his father for another minute, then said, "Listen, I've got to go." Pause. "Yeah, you, too."

Seeing him shove the phone in his hip pocket, Gabby said, "I'm sorry. I wasn't trying to eavesdrop, but I could hear you from the kitchen anyway."

"We didn't say anything private." Jack gave a crooked smile. "Dad was just accusing me of getting involved with you. He pointed out that I've never brought anyone involved with one of my investigations home with me before."

"Were any of them being hunted the way I am?"

He shrugged. "Maybe a gang member or two."

Gabby moistened her lips. "Did you try to defend yourself?"

"From Dad? No, why would I? He was right. I'm falling for you." His mouth twisted. "Have fallen."

Her chest cramped. "I'm still mad at you."

"I know." His throat worked. "I don't blame you. I had…tunnel vision. It made me stupid."

She nodded acknowledgment, struggling with contradictory emotions. It was hard to overcome feeling betrayed, but…she'd fallen for him, too. Wouldn't *she* be the stupid one if she held on to her grudge and threw away any chance at a future with the only man she'd ever felt this way about?

Yes.

"You won't lie to me again?"

"No. *God, no.*"

Gabby didn't even see him move, yet suddenly she was in his arms, holding him as tightly as he held her.

"This has been hell. Trying to keep you safe and knowing—" Jack broke off, his jaw muscles knotted.

"Knowing?" Her own eyes burned.

"You'd leave and I'd never see you again."

"I do have to find a job," she mumbled into his chest.

"There are a lot of colleges in commuting distance."

"I know." New confidence allowed her to lift her head and meet his eyes. "I've done some research."

He didn't blink for a long time as he studied her

face. Then he groaned, closed his eyes and bent forward to rest his forehead against hers. "Thank you."

"No, I'm the one who should be saying thank you, after you've come running to my rescue time after time."

He nuzzled her. "Let's call it good. No debts between us."

"No debts." She pushed up on tiptoe to press her mouth to his.

He took control of the kiss, which turned passionate and so urgent, Gabby wouldn't have minded if he'd laid her down on the hardwood floor and stripped her right now. But he didn't.

"Don't have any condoms with me," he growled, and steered her toward the staircase.

It was awfully hard to climb with his hands all over her, but from the sound of his breathing, the impact wasn't one-way.

Naturally, his bedroom was the last at the end of the hall, but they made it. They were barely beside his bed when Jack yanked back the covers and started stripping her even as she tried to pull up his sweatshirt and then unbuttoned and unzipped his jeans. He swore, clothes tangled with their limbs, and they finally made it into bed, naked.

They kissed until her head spun. Jack seemed to know exactly how and where to touch her. His fingers slid from one sensitive spot to another. She was already arching when he released her mouth and slid lower to suckle her breasts.

Gabby kneaded his chest and shoulders, frustrated

at her inability to reach that iron bar pressed against her thigh. Why did she have to be so short?

When he finally reached across her for the drawer in his bedside table, Gabby wrapped her fingers around him, squeezed and stroked and let him feel her fingernails. His hands were shaking as he put on the condom, and the heat in his eyes could have incinerated the sheets if his focus hadn't been so intensely on *her*.

The pleasure of joining was so powerful, she came with shocking speed. Jack drove her through the implosion and up again. There was nothing gentle or careful about this mating. That was not what she wanted, or what he needed. When he thrust a last time, hard, she came apart again. He collapsed on her, and Gabby didn't care if she ever breathed again.

AFTER THE BEST night of his life, Jack had never felt so energized…and so maddened by his inability to make any progress at all toward solving Colleen Ortiz's murder. It wasn't even lunchtime, and he had already called Gabby, needing the reassurance of hearing her voice. The sense of urgency that drove him was like a deep-seated itch he couldn't scratch, a just-heard drumbeat of warning.

She should be safe, but his gut said she wasn't.

Ric called to say he would be released from the hospital tomorrow morning. Yeah, he still felt like crap, but he could hire a visiting health aide to help with anything he couldn't manage. A couple of friends had invited him to recuperate at their homes, too. He hadn't decided.

Jack almost suggested Ric come to his place. He'd be company for Gabby. But something stopped him. He could be followed after picking up Ric, leaving the hospital and driving home. Ric was in no shape to get between his sister and another bullet, either.

"I think you should take one of them up on the offer," he said. "We're making progress—" He turned his head to be sure no one could hear his end of the conversation. "Gabby is helping me with some research. I don't like the idea of you alone in that house for now."

"You think I could be pressured to give away her whereabouts."

"We all have our breaking point."

A long pause. "I don't think I'd rest easy at home, anyway. Not after everything that's happened. Okay, I'll do that. But you'll stay in touch, won't you?"

"Count on it."

Jack ended the call and raked his fingers through his hair. Father Ambrose either didn't have a cell phone, or the diocese had chosen not to hand out that number. What if he was taking a two week vacation in the Caribbean? Filling in for an ill padre far enough from home he couldn't commute? He probably didn't check his voice mail as incessantly as people of a younger generation did.

Or didn't he want to talk about Colleen Ortiz?

Damn. Jack thought about calling the parish where

Father Ambrose now lived and occasionally served to beg for someone to hunt him down.

He glanced at his phone. It wasn't even lunchtime yet. Give the poor guy a chance. Maybe he'd had a full morning. Maybe he was talking to Gabby right that minute.

Nobody knew she was staying at his house, he reminded himself. Except Ric, of course. And Jack's father. Hell. How many friends here in town had Dad stayed in touch with? He'd have no reason to tell anyone what had been happening with the cold case, would he?

Jack's one accomplishment this morning was eliminating Sergeant Rutkowski as a suspect. He'd been talking to another detective he sometimes paired with on big cases. Mary Springer mentioned having worked Friday and Saturday both. Jack asked who else had been here, and she told him their sergeant was.

She'd grinned impishly. "His wife's sister and her family were with them for the four days. He said a little of the sister goes a long way, so he was hiding out. Really, all four of us at the station probably were, for our own reasons. None of us stepped foot out of the office. We ordered out for a big lunch—*not* turkey—and enjoyed the peace and quiet."

Relief flooded Jack. He *liked* the sergeant and had hated suspecting him.

Pinning down Chief Keller's whereabouts was inevitably a bigger challenge. Several layers of command separated Jack from the police chief. Until he'd asked to open the cold case, he'd had very little personal interaction with the man. Occasionally Keller dropped by to talk to Rutkowski. Otherwise, Jack saw their police chief giving statements during news conferences on TV, just like everyone else.

If the chief wanted to slip out, he had the advantage that the current city hall and police station were connected. He met frequently with the mayor or city council members. After all, Keller was a politician as much as anything, and probably spent half his time in those meetings.

Jack was good at strategy, but he couldn't figure out how to pin down where the police chief had been during fixed periods of time without sounding as if he was butting his nose in places it didn't belong. About all Jack had learned through common gossip was that Keller had taken the full four-day weekend, which meant he could have been anywhere.

What if he was upfront with Sergeant Rutkowski, who might be able to get answers to those questions without drawing unwanted notice?

Even imagining what Rutkowski would say to one of his detectives suspecting the chief of police of being a rapist and murderer had Jack wincing. It might be different if he could present even a grain of real evidence. The fact that Keller had left Leclaire High School after his sophomore year even though his parents didn't move away was damn suggestive timing. Add to that the fact that he'd stayed away until his father died, after which he immediately returned to Leclaire and took a job with LPD. As a puzzle piece, it dropped into place, cut to fit. But sure as hell, Dean Keller had told his story until it was completely believable.

They *needed* Father Ambrose.

Jack had run out of other strings to pull. The killer could well be someone he'd never considered, would have no way to identify. But his gut told him he was right. He just didn't know what he could do next, short of sitting in the parking lot watching for Keller to leave and then following him—which wasn't feasible.

Thoughts spinning in circles, he walked down the block to the nearby deli to buy a sandwich he could eat at his desk. Unfortunately, neither the brief activity nor the icy air outside cleared his mind.

He was stopped twice on his way in, once about another investigation, once by the patrol officer who'd handled the break-in at the Ortiz house and had just heard about the shooting. Jack filled him in on the continuing saga before taking the stairs rather than the elevator.

He'd intended to have his third or fourth cup of coffee with the sandwich, but saw the pot in the bullpen was down to sludge and crossed the hall to use the pop machine in the break room. Cold can in hand, he heard voices in the hall. Chief Keller and Rutkowski, he realized. Not prepared to produce another even semiconvincing update, he lurked a few feet inside the break room where he could see Keller's back blocking the detective bullpen doorway. His wait wasn't long. The police chief abruptly turned away and headed down the hall toward the elevators.

Feeling like a kid slinking around so Dad couldn't assign him a new chore, Jack crossed the hall without wasting time. He could see the chief striding away, and made sure to duck back into the bullpen before Keller happened to glance back.

At his desk, he started to unwrap his sandwich, but something niggled at him. Frowning, he turned to look toward the doorway to the hall. Had he ever seen Keller walk more than a few feet before? He had a distinctive stride—

Jack's phone rang, and his adrenaline spiked when he recognized the number.

"Detective Cowan here," he said. "Is this Father Ambrose?"

"It is. Given the questions, I thought it best to call you rather than the young lady." The priest had a strong voice that hadn't lost anything to age.

"Thank you. I don't know how much Gabby told you in her message, but I'm hoping you remember her mother, Colleen Ortiz."

"I do because that was such a distressing and delicate situation. I've asked myself many times over the years whether I made the right decision. To find out that she was later murdered… If I'd had the least idea…"

"I'm assuming what you learned is that she'd been raped."

"I wouldn't be able to tell you what she said in the confessional if she were alive, but given what Colleen's daughter said, I think I must."

"Colleen surely didn't blame herself for the rape to the extent that she felt she had to confess."

"No, her guilt came from her lies to her parents about where she was going. She wasn't a girl who did that kind of thing, but I gather she was completely infatuated with the boy. In the midst of telling me, she fell apart and it all came out. As…shattered as she was, she was absolutely determined not to go to the police. She already knew she wasn't pregnant, and she couldn't bear for her parents to know she'd been assaulted. She said that everyone would look at her differently, which is, regrettably, true. I had grave reservations about her thinking she could just put it behind her, but I couldn't ignore her wishes." The priest paused. "What a terrible thing to happen. Such a shock." He sighed. "I didn't know him or the family, since they didn't worship at St. Stephen's, but I had no difficulty locating them. I felt I was doing the right thing to take this to them. I don't believe Colleen could have borne seeing the boy every day at school. My meeting with the parents wasn't pleasant, of course. The mother was in complete denial, but his father agreed to withdraw him from the public school and send him to a boy's school, a military academy. He promised not to allow him to return to Leclaire. I…had the feeling that he'd already had some suspicions about his son."

Jack knew. *He knew*. Handsome and charming classmate well able to tempt a good girl to lie to her parents to meet him illicitly.

That rolling gait, the big, powerful body with a little softening around the middle told him enough.

Jack pushed back his desk chair and surged to his feet. Harshly, he said, "Father Ambrose, who was the boy?"

Chapter Seventeen

Dean Keller.

Who'd just gotten into an elevator either to ride up a floor to his office...or down, to leave the building.

Jack didn't know what else he'd said to the priest. What if Keller had been leaving? Electrified by fear, he knew only that he had to go home. Be there to protect Gabby.

He snatched his parka from the back of his chair and went straight to Rutkowski's office, rapping on the glass and entering without waiting for an invitation.

"Was Chief Keller going back up to his office?" Jack could only imagine what the sergeant saw on his face.

That had to be why he barely hesitated. "I don't know. You'd better have a good reason for asking." He picked up his phone and pushed a couple of buttons to route his call to the chief's office. "This is Rutkowski. The chief was just here. Is he back in his office yet?" Rutkowski's dark eyes met Jack's.

"Thanks." He dropped the receiver into the cradle. "He's gone for the day."

"I think he murdered Colleen Ortiz, and I'm damn sure he's trying to kill Gabby. I need to get home in case—"

"She's there?"

"Yeah." Jack's voice was hoarse with fear. "I've got to go."

"I'm going with you." The sergeant grabbed his holstered gun from a drawer, snapped it on his belt and swept up his coat on the way out of the office on Jack's heels.

Heads turned when the two men ran from the squad room and down the hall. Without discussion, they took the stairs two at a time. That saying about seeing your life pass before your eyes? Jack saw the life he wanted to have, complete with kids. The one he'd lose if he didn't stop the son of a bitch out to kill her.

Rutkowski leaped in on the passenger side of Jack's assigned police vehicle, buckling himself in as tires squealed and Jack accelerated toward the exit. He had his lights and siren on by the time he swerved onto the street.

"Explain."

Jack did, in a few short words. "I kept thinking I was crazy. He's my boss. He's a respected cop and has been chief for—"

"Seven years." The sergeant planted a hand on the dashboard as they rocketed through a yellow light.

"You're not arguing." How long had it been since Keller left the station? Could he be at Jack's house yet?

"I had a few thoughts that made me uncomfortable. Got the feeling you weren't telling us everything, either. Started wondering why that would be, and that brought back a memory of seeing Dean and Colleen together a few times in high school."

Jack fumbled his phone from his pocket and called Gabby.

Ring. Ring. Ring. Went on and on.

Rutkowski continued talking, but in his terror Jack had quit listening. A thought hit him and he called his father, putting his phone on speaker.

"Jack?"

"Did you tell anyone at all that Gabby is staying with me?"

"Nobody you need to worry about," his dad said, sounding surprised. "Your boss called me out of the blue last night, said you'd told him recently where I'd relocated to, and he was curious enough to decide to touch base. Hadn't heard from him in twenty years or more, but I must have mentioned him before."

"No," Jack said tersely. "I had no idea you knew him."

"After I was brought in for questioning about the Ortiz woman's death, he was friendly. Went out of his way to talk me through what was happening and reassure me that the interest in me was routine. Nothing to worry about. Like I said, we talked four or five times over the next few years, but we didn't have much in common."

"Did he ask where Gabby was staying?"

"Why would he when he knew? He said something like, 'Have to admire your boy for taking a witness home with him.' Said he was pleased you'd reopened that investigation, mentioned that you were keeping him in the loop." There was a silence Jack read as appalled. "You're not suggesting—"

Jack said a word he rarely used and cut his father off so he could redial Gabby.

Still no answer.

You're too late, said a voice in his head.

He wouldn't accept it.

FEELING CHILLED, GABBY went upstairs to put on a sweater. While she was there, she used the bathroom. Washing her hands, she leaned closer to the mirror to study herself. Wow. Apparently, extreme stress had more impact on her appearance than all the happiness in the world could. Where was the glow Jack had claimed to see when she was able to tell him that Ric had regained consciousness and was going to be fine? Shouldn't a night of astonishing sex with a man who hadn't quite told her that he loved her, but had come really, really close be giving her a glow?

Instead, her eyes were sunken and bruised-looking and her skin pasty. Maybe she should think about applying some makeup before Jack got home.

As if he hadn't already seen her this morning.

She made a face at herself, dried her hands and reached for her phone...only to realize she must have left it downstairs. *Dumb.* What if she'd missed Father Ambrose's call? Or Ric had taken a downturn?

She hurried toward the staircase and started down. The last place she'd been was the kitchen, where she'd rinsed out her coffee mug after who-knew-how-many refills. She could have set the phone down on the counter...

The familiar ringtone came to her. She probably couldn't reach it in time to catch the call, but—

At the sound of glass breaking, she froze with one foot hovering in midair.

That had to be at the back of the house, she thought, with a calm clarity that had separated itself from her panic. If she could get to her phone... But what if he was coming in the kitchen window?

A strange rattling made her hesitate. Blinds. She could all but see a hand reaching in through a broken pane on the French doors that led from the dining room out to a deck. Jack had left the blinds closed, as he had on all the other windows.

What if she ran for the kitchen, waited until she heard the intruder enter, and ran *out* the kitchen door? She might have a few seconds until the intruder realized that Jack had installed a sliding lock at the top of the French doors.

Splintering wood gave her all the answer she needed. He'd kicked his way inside, and if she went that direction, she'd pass within sight of him.

Upstairs. She felt her way backward with one foot before she overcame that instinctive need to mindlessly flee.

A voice whispered, *Wrong way.*

Already tiptoeing down the last few steps and rushing around the wall that framed the staircase and formed an alcove in the living room, she knew the voice was right. Upstairs, she'd be trapped. Worse yet, there was nowhere to hide. Jack was either a neat freak or just hadn't collected much yet. Under the bed might work playing hide-and-seek with kids, but not for hiding from a killer.

She could run for the front door, but unlocking the dead bolt would make noise. By the time she fled out onto the porch—if she got that far—he'd be on her. He could pump a couple of bullets into her back, go out the way he'd come and be long gone before anyone in a passing car noticed the woman's body half-fallen down the front porch steps.

The space under the stairs. Not really a closet, but unlike the rest of the house, it *was* cluttered, partly with the boxes holding her mother's stuff. The two that were definitely thrift store bound sat beside the front door, but Jack had shoved the others in there as well.

Rather than a door, it had a sliding panel someone might miss noticing. It allowed an opening just wide enough for a person to crawl in. She couldn't remember how much noise the panel made when it .was moved.

Didn't matter. She was out of choices.

"Get a unit to the house," Rutkowski snapped into the radio. "Sirens, lights. Backup preferable. Do you hear me?" The obscenities he uttered told Jack all he needed to know. Dispatch didn't think they could get a patrol car to his house any faster than he and Rutkowski would reach it.

"Might be better," the sergeant muttered. "We have some rookies that barely shave. Would some kid, confronted by the chief, be able to shoot him?"

Jack hit redial, saw the light turning red ahead of him and barely slowed enough to be sure cross traffic had seen the emergency lights. Then he accelerated again.

"Try calling Keller," he suggested. If he hadn't thought to turn off his phone, the ringing could warn Gabby.

Rutkowski did. "Straight to voice mail. Unbelievable."

Jack was driving at unsafe speeds for the residential streets they'd reached, but he didn't care. No kid would be out riding his bike when the temperature was still below freezing.

"How far?" his companion asked.

"Two minutes," he said grimly. Too far.

THE INTRUDER HADN'T made a sound since he'd stepped into the dining room. If only the wood floors in this old house weren't so solid, she thought in despair as she eased open the panel. She could hear it scraping, but the sound was faint.

That was wide enough. She bent to whisk inside, had to stretch to step over one of the boxes and then reach back to flatten her hand on the panel. *Push it back, slow, slow.* He might be in the living room.

It was pitch black now in this cubby. To move without knocking something over or even tripping and falling, she had to depend on her memory from looking over Jack's shoulder as he put the boxes in here and from the brief moment when she entered.

The space was the same depth as the width of the staircase, but extended at least eight feet in length, the far wall butting up to the utility room.

The one oddity in here was an indoor hammock Jack must have found he wasn't using. The two-piece frame leaned against the wall, the net heaped beside it. She could pull it over herself, huddle beneath just as she had hidden beneath the sheets in the laundry room when she was a little girl.

In plain sight.

Her teeth wanted to chatter, but she clenched her jaw.

Yes, she'd try hiding under the hammock, but she needed a weapon. She couldn't just crouch there with no way to fight back. Jack had plenty of sports equipment—a wooden baseball bat would have been ideal—but he kept all that out in the garage. If she could have gotten out there…

Not a chance.

Built of solid wood, the frame for the hammock was too unwieldy.

A *squeak* came to her ears. On a step right above her…but was he going up, or down?

Her mind jumped around. How had he found out she was staying here? Then an awful chill struck her.

The only person Jack had told, to her knowledge, was his father. What if he'd murdered Colleen after all? He'd have had time to drive from Oregon if he'd set out right away after talking to his son.

Or he could have been here all along. With a cell phone, you couldn't tell.

If Jack had to arrest his own father… She shuddered.

Think. If only she had her phone. *Well, I don't.*

Wait. What about the bookends packed in with the books? Both pairs were heavyweight. The painted, cast-iron fleur-de-lis had jagged edges as well as enough weight to hurt someone, but the other set, leaping cats carved out of marble, might be even better.

But where were the books? Which box held which set of bookends?

She gathered up the hammock and draped it over herself so that she could sink down beneath it at any moment, and carefully opened the flaps of a box she thought held books.

Yes!

The next *creak* came close enough to cause her to hold her breath. Where was that? Like most old houses, this one didn't have a coat closet. The nearest interior door was at the entrance to the kitchen, and it had been standing open.

She strained to hear even a whisper of sound.

The panel not two feet from her vibrated.

JACK HAD CUT the siren a couple of minutes ago. He and Rutkowski had debated coming in with siren wailing versus sneaking up to the house—and had gone with sneaking. It was too late to scare Keller away before he got into the house. Now, chances were too good he'd already popped a lock or broken a window.

First, though, Jack did one sweep around the back side of his block.

The black Cadillac Escalade registered to his name was parked in a driveway on the next block, in front of a house with a For Sale sign in the yard.

Jack had wanted to be wrong. Now he knew he wasn't.

"You ready?" he asked.

"Damn straight."

Three doors from his house, he jerked to a stop. By the time he put the gearshift in Park and yanked out the key, Rutkowski had sprung out, pushed the door not quite shut to avoid a slamming sound, and was running full out for the open space between Jack's house and his next-door neighbor's. The plan was for him to slip in the gate and enter the house from the back. Jack had responsibility for the front—and, he hoped, drawing Keller's attention and fire.

He sprinted for the near end of the porch, leaped to catch the edge of the broad flat top of the railing and hauled himself up and over. He tried to land lightly, but heard an inevitable thud and went still.

His phone vibrated.

entry french doors going in

He typed 15 secs.

The glass in both windows was intact. He sidled

toward the nearest one, cursed himself for having left all the blinds closed, and moved fast until he was past it to the front door. No reason Keller would linger in Jack's home office.

He'd give a lot to be able to see in. To have even a hint of what was happening inside. The house was completely silent.

Nudging at him was the fear that Gabby hadn't answered her phone because she was already dead— but if that was so, why hadn't Keller already slipped out the back and driven away? No, Jack had to believe she'd had a chance to hide. But where? The old-fashioned kitchen pantry had some decent cupboards, but he guessed Keller had entered through the back, which would likely have cut off the kitchen. And, unfortunately, the garage, where there were more options for hiding—and some potential weapons.

He slid the key into the lock and turned it. Tiny click. Grabbed the doorknob and took a deep breath.

Go.

THE PANEL ABRUPTLY slid as far open as it went, letting light in. Gabby hunched beneath the rough striped fabric of the hammock. She could just see out around the edge, to an ominous dark shape blocking the light from the living room. He crouched to peer in. For a terrifying moment, she was four again. *Mommy screaming, blood splashing, grunts from the man stabbing, stabbing, stabbing. Mommy silent.*

Can't look, can't look. Have to.

He's looking at me.

Her head swam. She inhaled soundlessly and clutched the marble bookend. She wanted to smash his head. She wanted *him* to suffer.

"I know you're in here," he said. "Let's see. What about—"

Pop. Pop. A box jumped.

"No?"

The front door slammed open and, still at a crouch, he spun to face the threat.

Gabby pushed off the hammock, jumped over the box and ducked to avoid hitting her head. Then she swung the marble cat as hard as she could for the monster's head. It was like striking a jack-o'-lantern on Halloween. No, a pumpkin with innards intact. Brains. *Smash, squish.*

The sensations mixed with gunfire, men yelling, glass breaking—and something knocking her backward. *He* was down. Puzzled, Gabby raised her gaze to Jack, bending over the man—and then she dropped to her knees, to her butt, and everything went black.

GABBY KNEW FROM the smell alone that she was in the hospital. Lying still, she did a brief evaluation. Toes wriggled. Fingers, too. But her shoulder hurt. That stirred memories of waking up to a strange woman's face hovering over her, the woman assuring her that she was fine, the surgery had been successful, she could just rest now. She'd seen Jack a couple of times, too, hadn't she?

Gabby opened her eyes and blinked a few times. She felt truly awake this time.

"Back with us?"

She knew Jack's voice, and turned her head. He stood beside the bed looking down at her, every line in his face carved deep.

"How do you feel?"

"I…" She worked her mouth, trying to come up with some saliva. "Okay."

"Here." He sat next to her and helped her take a few sips from a cup of water.

Then they looked at each other.

"You're not supposed to leap up when guns are being fired," he observed, almost mildly.

She wasn't fooled. "He was going to shoot you."

"He did shoot me."

"What?" She struggled to sit up.

He gently pressed her back. "Hey. Stay put. I was wearing a vest."

"Oh." Gabby absorbed that. "Did you shoot me?"

"I'm afraid so."

Well, he was right. She'd sort of asked for it. Anyway, that's not what was most important right now. "He wasn't your father, was he?"

It was Jack's turn to say, "What?" Then he shook his head. "No. Why would you think…" He made the connection. "Because I told him you were staying with me. No, of course it wasn't him, but he told the wrong person." If anything, the grooves in his forehead were even deeper. "Dean Keller killed your mother. He's the police chief. *Was* the police chief. My boss."

Her mind still wasn't sharp enough to consider the ramifications of that. "You shot him."

"I did." His blue eyes were momentarily cold. "Killed him, too—if your blow to his head hadn't already done the job."

"I hope it did. As I crouched there, one of the last things I thought was that I wanted to *hurt* him."

Jack took her hand. The warm strength felt so good.

"I can't even imagine how you handled that, having to hide from him a second time," he said, voice deep. "You're amazing."

"I...had a flashback or two," she admitted. "But... I was determined not to be so helpless again. It would have been nice if you'd kept a baseball bat or, I don't know, a great big knife in the closet, but no."

His hand tightened until the grip was almost painful, but he also managed a crooked smile. "Weapon in every closet from now on. Although you did find one. I didn't pay attention to those bookends, but that was a heavy sucker."

"Marble," she said with satisfaction.

"Damn, Gabby." He bent forward and nuzzled her, then gave her a feather-soft kiss. "I've never been so scared in my life."

She gave a tiny nod. She couldn't say the same, and he knew why.

"This is too soon to push you, but..." His chest rose and fell with a long, pained breath. "If you'll give me a chance, I'm willing to go wherever you want to live. Staying in Leclaire can't have a lot of appeal. I can get a job anywhere."

Now that he'd straightened, she searched his face and found only desperate sincerity. He meant it. He'd really uproot himself for her.

Gabby tried to smile, knew her lips trembled. "Ric's here. And…if you're not in trouble—"

"For shooting and killing the police chief, you mean?" He grimaced. "I'm on administrative leave, which is normal after a shooting. My direct boss, Sergeant Rutkowski, was with me, which helps. No matter what, no one investigating can deny the son of a bitch was trying to kill you. If we had to try him for your mom's murder—" He stopped himself. "Guess that's not happening."

It wasn't. Because the man was dead.

Later she might have to grapple with the knowledge that she might have killed someone, but now—

She had to dampen her lips. "If…if you mean what I think you're saying, I wouldn't mind trying to stay in Leclaire. If I can't get a job, well—"

"Anywhere," Jack said huskily. "Anywhere at all. Anytime." His lips met hers.

This kiss expressed so much: passion, tenderness, commitment. And it was also brief, because Jack was determined not to hurt her.

They held hands and talked quietly, sharing plans and promises until she drifted back to sleep.

* * * * *

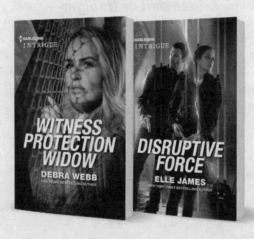

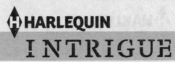

The narrow mountain road ended at the edge of a rock cliff.
It wasn't as if Ford Cardwell had forgotten that. No, when
he saw where he was, he knew it was why he'd taken this
road and why he was going so fast as he approached the
sheer vertical drop to the rocks far below. It would have
been so easy to keep going, to put everything behind him,
to no longer feel pain.

Pine trees blurred past as the pickup roared down the
dirt road to the nothingness ahead. All he could see was
sky and more mountains off in the distance. Welcome back
to Montana. He'd thought coming home would help. He'd
thought he could forget everything and go back to being the
man he'd been.

His heart thundered as he saw the end of the road coming
up quickly. Too quickly. It was now or never.

The words sounded in his ears, his own when he was
young. He saw himself standing in the barn loft looking out
at the long drop to the pile of hay below. Jump or not jump.
It was now or never.

He was within yards of the cliff when his cell phone rang. He slammed on his brakes. An impulsive reaction to the ringing in his pocket? Or an instinctive desire to go on living?

The pickup slid to a dust-boiling stop, his front tires just inches from the end of the road. Heart in his throat, he looked out at the plunging drop in front of him.

His heart pounded harder. Just a few more moments—a few more inches—and he wouldn't have been able to stop in time.

His phone rang again. A sign? Or just a coincidence? He put the pickup in Reverse a little too hard and hit the gas pedal. The front tires were so close to the edge that for a moment he thought the tires wouldn't have purchase. Fishtailing backward, the truck spun away from the precipice.

Ford shifted into Park and, hands shaking, pulled out his still-ringing phone. As he did, he had a stray thought. How rare it used to be to get cell phone coverage here in the Gallatin Canyon of all places. Only a few years ago the call wouldn't have gone through.

Without checking to see who was calling, he answered it, his hand shaking as he did. He'd come so close to going over the cliff. Until the call had saved him.

"Hello?" He could hear noises in the background. *"Hello?"* He let out a bitter chuckle. A robocall had saved him at the last moment, he thought, chuckling to himself.

But his laughter died as he heard a bloodcurdling scream coming from his phone.

Don't miss
Trouble in Big Timber *by B.J. Daniels,*
available June 2021 wherever
Harlequin Intrigue books and ebooks are sold.

Harlequin.com

HIEXP0521